The Lick

By:

Nico Harswell

26 you

Thank you so much
for the Support!

Nico Harswell

Nico Harswell

ISBN-9798615455230

Book Production: Crystell Publications
You're The Publisher, We're Your Legs
We Help You Self Publish Your Book

BOP E-mail ONLY – cleva@crystalstell.com
E-Mail – minkassitant@yahoo.com
Website: www.crystellpublications.com
(405) 414-3991

Printed in the USA

ACKNOWLEDGEMENTS

First of all, I would like to say Thank You to my Lord and Savior Jesus Christ. You've been there from the beginning. You told me in Isiah 54:7 that as long as I believe on Your name: "No weapon formed against me shall prosper."

Thank you to my family. Mom, thank you for always seeing through my eyes. Thank you to my bro and sisters for their continuous love and support.

To my daughter, Damiria, Daddy loves you. To my son, Damian, I'm proud of you. Continue to get educated.

To all my nieces and nephews, (grands included), I love yall!

To any and everyone else that may have helped me along my journey, Thank You!

If I didn't call you by name, please don't judge me. Understand that when Jonah was in the belly of the fish, his objective was simple… Getting the hell out!!!

If you have a special place in my life, I don't have to name you. You already have your place in my heart.

R.I.P.

My father, James "Sonny" Harswell, Sr. My brother, Calvin "Packy" Harswell. My nephew, Marquise "4-4" Wadley.

To my writers … J-Mac, Nathaniel, and all others … "Preciate ya."

Georgia Boi Publications for life …

Rules of The Game

1. I came into this organization as one - but now my life and the life of the organization and my new family rests upon my shoulders. We live as one and we die as one.

2. Never allow your emotions to make a decision that's too deep for your pockets.

3. I will not let the hate I have for my enemy allow me to make a selfish decision that will cause the organization to suffer.

4. To order death on a member of the organization is to order death on myself.

5. Never put anything before family. When a choice has to be made that involves family - Always choose family.

6. Never allow an excuse to be a reason for your failure.

7. My word is Bond and Bond is life. Before my word fails, I will give my life.

8. To steal from the organization is to steal from myself. We are one.

9. Never share family business with an outsider.

10. In the heat of a battle, never abandon a family member. We fight until victory or death.

PROLOGUE

Tony looked at his watch. It was 3:27am. This was the moment of truth. It was now or never. He looked over at Maine, who seem to have a look in his eyes that could've easily been mistaken for weakness. But Tony knew there was nothing weak about his partner in crime. Maine was a true thoroughbred that would ride or die until the end of time.

"Three minutes!" Tony said as he looked around the dark parking lot.

"Are you sure we're gonna be able to get the front of the truck?" Maine impatiently asked.

"One hundred percent! I told you the old men smoke like a train."

At 4:00am the Wells Fargo truck turned into the far end of the parking lot. Tony and Maine hungrily watched as it slowly made its way to the front of the building.

"Let's do this!" Tony grasped as he lowered the ski-mask on his face.

They both exited the stolen car and paused as a tall, skinny, white male climbed from the passenger seat and walked to the back of the truck. He waved his hand to his partner' and the large door begin to open.

Stan Jefferson and Buddy 'Bud' Tinsley had been partners for over fifteen years. They delivered and picked up money for Wells Fargo. They praised themselves, because they never had any problems and most of all, they were always on time.

"Alright, Bud, fire'em up if you got'em," Stan said as he pulled out a pack of Marlboro light 100's.

Bud rolled down the bulletproof window to let the smoke out, as he pulled his second cigarette from the half empty pack of Basie's.

"This is the last stop, Stan," Bud yelled as the filter dangled between his lips.

"That's right!" Stan snapped. "If these doors open on time, I'll be watching the sunrise from Lake Sinclair."

"You going fishing!" Bud shouted with joy towards the back of the truck. Stan didn't answer.

Bud thought maybe he had climbed into the back of the truck to unload the money but didn't remember feeling the tilt of the truck whenever Stan hopped on back. He took another pull from his cigarette, then turned to blow the smoke out of the window. He was sixty-seven years old, and ten years pass his retirement date, but couldn't stand to sit at home. His wife, Lizzy would call his name non-stop, and just the thought of it made Bud reach for another cancer stick. He looked around for the pack and noticed it fell on the floor.

"Damn!" he whispered to himself as he stretched his old bones to pick it up. When he finally raised his head, Bud was face to face with the silencer that sat at the end of Tony's 9mm Beretta. "Easy old man," Tony stated as he opened the door carefully.

"I ain't trying hurt nobody. Just let me handle my business and be on my way," he continued.

Tony averted his eyes towards the shotgun that was still locked in the case. The two old white men had been doing this so long, they didn't think about their own safety anymore.

"Look, son! You don't want to do this. You're making a big mistake," Bud pleaded.

"You're right!" Tony gritted. 'PFF!' the pistol whispered as the bullet tore half of the old man face off.

Tony jumped down, walked to the back of the truck and then climbed inside. Maine already had Stan tied up. He looked at his watch.

"4:04, we got six minutes to load as much cash as we can," he told his friend.

Tony and Maine carefully loaded the bags of money, watching to avoid the dye filled bags. His inside connection told him to avoid all the bags with red serial numbers.

"4:09!" Tony said as he hurled the duffle bag across his shoulder.

"What about him?" Maine asked, pointing at Stan.

Tony turned and looked at the old man. His eyes were bulged wide open and sweat was running down his face. He pulled out the pistol 'PFF' the gun spit as the silencer held back the loud cry. Stan's body slumped over on to a pile of money bags.

"I thought you said you wasn't gonna hurt anybody," Maine asked as he grabbed another bag of money.

"I changed my mind, now let's go! " Tony made his order and made their exit.

Nico Harswell

CHAPTER ONE

The After Party

Six months earlier:

Tony and Maine stood on the wall in Club 3DL watching the V.I.P. area. A major hustler was throwing a birthday bash. Women filled the club with as little clothes as possible on, each trying to get the attention of a baller.

"Look T, there goes Mindy," Maine pointed out to his boy.

"I see her," Tony replied, trying to be conspicuous as he rubbed his chin. "Damn! She's still fine," he mumbled, looking at his boy. "Yo chill, Big Dog! I'm bout to go holla at her."

"Bet that!" Maine said as he watched his best friend go after his high school sweetheart.

The club was packed, making it hard for Tony to move through the crowd. He bumped his way around, until he finally caught up with her near the steps of the V.I.P. section. "Mindy!" he shouted over the music.

Mindy Valentine was just entering the club. She did not like the crowd but had promised her BFF that she would show up. Maurice Goines was having a birthday bash, and had sent her an invitation through Meka, as well as a dozen of roses to her job. Mindy knew that Tweet liked her, but the streets had captured his heart long ago.

As she stepped across the floor, she could feel the eyes on her. Mindy was five feet even; she was 110 lbs. and had a nice figure. Her mother was white, and her father was black, which gave her a flawless caramel complexion. Mindy had a natural, silky, blackhead of curly hair that hung to her plump butt. She was just about to enter V.I.P. when she heard her name being called. Seconds later, she looked around only to find Tony walking up.

"What's up Mindy? What are you doing out?"

"Nothing much, just came to chill with my girl for a little while," she replied.

"Well, I was wondering when you were gonna let a nigga take you out."

"Tony – I told you you we're like family. I don't see us that way."

"Mindy! We are not family, just one date."

"Let me think about it first," she told him as she turned to walk through the velvet ropes. Tony stood watching her for a couple of seconds, then she went back to join Maine.

Maurice "Tweet" Goines was turning twenty-one years old. He has been living the dream of most guys twice his age. Not only was he the son of Dublin, Georgia's drug kingpin, Larry "LG" Goines, but he'd made a name for himself as well.

Tweet slept with a different girl every night, just like his father. Lil Wayne said it best, when he said, 'Like Father Like Son.' But with all his fly cars and all the money he had, there was still one girl that wouldn't give him the time or day.

He drank out the bottle of Grey Goose as he watched her walk in the club and turn heads. To say she was a dime would have been an understatement. This bitch was bad. As she made it to the V.I.P. section Tweet watched as Tony walked up on her.

"Broke ass nigga!" he said to himself, closely watching her.

Tweet was off to the side, watching Mindy walk through V.I.P. like she was lost. It was the perfect time to strike, and he took advantage of the chance.

"Mindy, over here!" he shouted, standing in the chair to get her attention.

"I'm looking for Meka," she yelled over the music, continuing to look around the room.

"Shit! Meka ain't got shit on my peoples," he replied as he held up a stack of money. "Come chill with a real nigga. "

"I'm good!" she dismissively said, walking past his booth.

"Mindy! Mindy! Over here," Meka shouted over the noise.

"I thought you were gonna wait on me at the door."

"Girl, you know Zach be tripping," Meka told her, guiding her towards the area she had been chilling in.

Zachary "Zach" Brown was Meka's boyfriend and the righthand man of Tweet. Unlike Mindy, Meka reaped all the benefits from fucking a hustler. Zach spent thousands on her, and she let him. When she was young, her mother taught her that whenever she got out of bed with a nigga, make sure she was "good" between her legs and pocketbook. If nothing else, Meka made sure she did her job well. Actually, she ensured that the best gold digger in the city didn't have shit on her.

Tameka Williams, whom most referred to as Meka, was dark skinned, opposite of Mindy but had natural hazel eyes. She wore her hair short with different styles, and tonight she was rocking the mohawk.

"Mindy, I want you to meet my co-worker, Jessica.

"Hey!" Mindy greeted, looking at the girl. She was pretty, but nowhere near her and Meka.

"What's up? I heard a lot about you," Jessica said as she gave Mindy a once over as well.

"Well, I hope it was good," Mindy shyly stated.

"It was all good."

"Okay bitches!" Meka stepped in. "Let's ball the fuck out!"

* * * *

Tony and Maine stood across the club watching the crowd. Maine was looking for some late-night pussy, but Tony kept his eyes on Mindy. He watched as Tweet pulled on her arm, tryna get her to dance with him. He clenched his teeth as he felt the blood begin to boil in his veins.

"Bra! What you staring at?" Maine asked.

"That pussy ass nigga Tweet. He thinks just cause he got a little paper, he can fuck anybody he wants."

"Man, you know them hoes gonna flock to that check. That's why I can't wait to get my paper up. I'mma make' em feel me."

"You right. When I get my paper up, that's the first nigga I'mma shit on," Tony stated as he continued to watch them interact.

They stood on the wall sharing a blunt, as they both conversed and were in a slight daze, dreaming about getting rich. When the lights came on, you could hear the D-Jay shout, "That's it! Until the next time, Happy Birthday, Tweet!"

The crowd begin to cheer. As Tweet and his crew piled out, Tony and Maine made it out the club and was standing with the on-lookers. Tony saw Mindy and headed her way. He wanted to tell her good night. Just as he was within a few feet from her, she was pulled away. He watched as Tweet tried to pull her into his limo. Mindy was pulling in the opposite direction, trying to free herself. Wanting his way, Tweet begin to pull harder clearly unaware of the fact that the alcohol made him hurt her. Seeing the expression on her face, Tony rushed to her aide.

"Let her the fuck go!" He snapped as he freed Mindy from Tweet's grip.

"Well, well, well ... if it ain't this mutha' fuckin, broke ass, phony Tony to the rescue," Tweet said, looking Tony over from head to toe in disgust.

"My name is Tony," he corrected Tweet.

"I don't give a fuck ... Phony Tony," he said as his crew burst into laughter.

"Mindy, are you ok?" Tony asked.

"Yeah," she said, giving him a nod, while also rubbing her arm.

"And if she ain't, what can you do about it? You can't buy her a fucking band-aid, Phony Tony."

Tony rushed in to grab Tweet but was stopped by his crew.

"I got yo Phony Tony, fuck boy! Pick the time and place, and I promise I'll be there. I'll be there mutha' fucka!" Tony yelled as Maine pulled him away.

"Chill baby boy. You can handle this another time," Maine told him as he tried to calm his partner.

"That nigga gonna pay," Tony continued to rant loud enough for Tweet to hear.

"Sorry, fuck nigga. I'm already paid!" Tweet screamed, throwing a wad of money into the crowd, right as his limo pulled off.

* * * *

"Mindy! Mindy get up!" Her mother shouted as she stood over her. "You're gonna be late for work."

"I'm off today, ma," Mindy groggily replied.

"Well, if you're off, why in the hell does your schedule on the refrigerator say you work Sunday, which is today. According to that sheet of paper, you work from ten until closing?"

Sarah Valentine stood there looking at her daughter waiting for her reply. She had been around the block a time or two, and if she thought she could pull a fast one over on her, she'd better think again. She was white, but that was only the color of her skin. Sarah had wild out with the best of them. She had lived to smoke, drink and party, but when she got pregnant with Mindy, she changed her life.

Her childhood had been tough. Her mother was a crackhead, and she didn't know her father. As she stared at her daughter, she thought back to when she was a child, and how she screamed for her mother.

Sarah was only six years old. She climbed out of her bed and walked to her mother's bedroom door. She could hear screaming as if someone was fighting. She cracked the door open, and she could see her mother on her hands and knees with her face buried in a pillow. The smell was terrible.

"Oh God!" her mother screamed. "Take it out! You're hurting me."

Sarah watched as, "The Milk Man", which Mommy called him, hurt her mother. "Leave her alone!" she shouted.

The Milk Man looked around at her with lust filled eyes. "If you let me taste that, too. I got something extra for you," he said to her mother, eyeing Sarah's small body.

"No ...no! That's my baby," her mother protested.

"Look at what I got for you," he said, showing her a huge piece of crack.

She looked at the drugs, then back at Sarah. "Come here baby. Come let The Milk Man make you feel good."

Sarah thought of all the times her mother watched as different men abused her body. She promised herself if she ever had a daughter, she would love her like a mother should – and with all her heart and soul.

"Young lady, get out that bed, now!" She ordered as she turned and walked away.

Mindy crawled out the bed. When she raised up, she felt a sharp pain in her arm. She looked down at the bruise. "Stupid!" she said to herself as she thought about the night before.

Tweet had been so drunk that he almost broke her arm trying to pull her into his car. She almost allowed herself to be pulled in to stop the pain, but out of 'nowhere Tony popped up and freed her from his grip.

She watched as Tony was mocked by Tweet and his crew. Why did she go to the stupid party anyway? She looked at her alarm clock, it read 9:15 a.m. She had forty-five minutes to get to work. She stepped in the hot shower and let the water wash away the memories of last night.

Afterwards, Mindy stood in the mirror with her yellow shirt, black pants and Ronald McDonald visor. After she was satisfied with her look, she headed out the door.

"Love you," she said before leaving out.

"Love you more," Sarah shouted back, loudly echoing over the TV that played in the background.

CHAPTER TWO

"A TASTE OF THE GOOD LIFE"

Tony rolled over and picked up his phone, "Yeah," he mumbled still half asleep.

"Man, get up!" Maine shouted.

"Damn, why you shouting in my ear? What time is it anyway?"

"It's almost twelve but check this out. My cousin called and said he's on the Greyhound from New York. He wants me to pick him up at two o'clock."

"Okay, now what the fuck that gotta do with me!?"

"Bra, on G." He told me he got ta plan that's gonna put some serious bread in our pockets. We're about to be straight gangsta."

"Maine, I ain't selling no dope. That ain't my stello."

"I don't know what it is, but I'm tired of being broke. When I scoop him up, we're gonna come through."

"Bet that on, G," Tony said as he raised up out of the bed.

"On G, my nigga! "Maine seriously replied, ending the call.

Tony walked into the bathroom and took a well needed piss, and then he hopped in the shower. As he thought about the events from the previous night, he put the water on full blast. *I can't believe Tweet played me like a real sucker in front of the whole club, not to mention Mindy*, he thought. Furious, he could feel his blood boiling in his veins as his rage resurfaced.

"I got yo phony Tony, pussy nigga," he said to himself as he began to get dressed.

On his way out the door, Tony walked past the kitchen table and picked up a drumstick from a basket of fresh fried chicken.

"You need to get a job, to help pay these bills," his sister shouted.

"You need to get the fuck off my back!" he screamed back, walking out the door.

Tony lived with his sister in a Section Eight apartment that was provided by the government. When Tina became pregnant at the age of fifteen, her mother put her out. Her mother was upset because the rumor had it that the young nigga, she had dicking her down at night was also dicking Tina down while she was at work. For that reason alone, she hated her daughter and hated the baby even more.

When Tina reached out for her help during her pregnancy, her mother would call her every low-down, dirty word she could think of, and then she'd slammed the phone down in her face. With nowhere else to turn, she called D.F.A.C.S. (Department of Family and Children Services) on herself. They took her in and placed her in a home until she had her son. While in their custody, they groomed her until she turned seventeen, then they gave her an apartment, along with all the government benefits she needed to adequately take care of her son.

After nights of starving with his mother, Tony moved in with his sister. At first, she let him in with open arms, but as times got harder, she demanded that he step up to the plate and help her.

Tony walked up the street eating on the drumstick. When he was done, he tossed the bone to a stray dog, who gulped it down in one bite. The dog had followed him from the time he turned the corner of his sister's building. When he made it to the corner, he saw Maine's bubble Caprice coming down the street.

He threw his hands up, causing Maine to pull over with the stranger.

"What's up my G?" Maine said, reaching across the seat to give him dap.

"What up, gangsta?" Tony replied.

"This Rod, my cousin I told you about from New York."

"What's up, homie," Tony said, holding out his fist for a bump.

"What's happening, son. Yo, I heard mad shit about you."

"Oh yeah," Tony stated, tripping off his New York accent.

"Yo! That's on my word. Son say you on fly with the hoop game."

"I'm alright!"

Tony was the leading scorer in the McDonald's All-American game two years straight. His basketball skills were raw talent. Just to get him ready to play, the coaches provided him with a new pair of Air Jordan's every year. He always played basketball long enough to get the shoes, then skipped all practices. He was the type to only show up and out on game night, which resulted in him leading both teams in scoring, each time he played.

"Where to?" Maine asked.

"I'm hungry then a mutha' fucka," Rod said.

Tony was hungry too; however, he didn't have any money. He sat in the back seat and watched as Maine waited for an answer.

"Yo, that's Subway," Rod stated, pointing at the deli that was sandwiched in the middle of the small plaza.

Maine whipped into the parking lot, almost missing the turn. Rodney "Rod" Turner was from Brooklyn, New York, and he loved to visit his family in, "The Country", which is what he called it. Things in Dublin was slow compared to the fast life of the city. When they turned into the small plaza, he immediately noticed the *Andy's Finance Company* a few stores down.

Rod was a straight up stick-up kid and got his money the old school way – laying 'em down. He looked back at Tony before making his move.

"Yo son, you ain't hungry?" he asked, waiting for him to get out of the car.

"Nah, I ain't hungry."

"Here son," Rod said as he peeled off a twenty-dollar bill from his stack. "Grab me the foot-long steak sub on flat bread and get you something too. I'm about to go next door to check this joint out," he said, pointing at the movie gallery. "Tell Maine to pull over and pick me up," he continued as he took off down the sidewalk.

Rod walked in *Andy's Finance Company* and locked the door behind him. There was only one old white lady behind the counter. She had on thick glasses that was covered by strands of silver hair.

He slipped on his mask and eased up to the counter.

"May I help you?" she asked as she turned to face the customer.

"You scream, you die," Rod whispered. "Now sit down on the floor."

The old woman strained as her bones popped to make it to the floor. When she had nearly touched the floor, Rod gave her a push. As she tumbled the rest of the way down, causing a loud thump, he watched as she lost her glasses. As she settled on the floor, he leaned down and whispered.

"Yo, I'm gonna ask you one time. How many people in the

back?"

"Just my son, Andy," she stated in fear.

Rod took out a roll of duct tape. He placed a strip across her mouth seconds before wrapping her arms behind her back. He cut the phone cord and looked around the room, spotting her cellphone on the counter. He grabbed it and tossed it in the trash bin, then slowly made his way down the hall. He could hear a voice coming from the first room he got to. He peeped into the room through the crack in the door and spotted his victim.

Andy was on the 1-800-Hot-Line listening, as the live link operator told him all the things she wanted to do to his three-hundred-pound body.

"You know I will," he groggily replied with his eyes closed. As Andy continued to stroke his dick, Rod walked up to the desk. He pointed the pistol at Andy's head, while pushing the button to end the call.

"No nut for you, slob!" he told him with a disgusted look on his face.

At the sight of the gun, Andy jumped out of the chair.

"I... I... I!" he stuttered.

"If you don't sit your fat ass down, you'll make the front page of tomorrows paper," Rod growled. "Now, I'm gonna ask you one mutha' fuckin time, son – Where's the fuckin money?"

Andy looked at the black mask, as he pointed to the desk drawer. "It's in there."

Rod pulled the drawer open and saw rows of neatly stacked bills. He pulled a bag out of his pocket and quickly begin to stuff the money inside.

"Where's the rest of it, you fat fuck!?" Rod demanded.

"That's it!" Andy cried, hoping he would only leave with the money he had taken in today.

"Five… four... three," Rod counted off as he loaded a bullet into the chamber. "Two," he continued.

"Wait!" Andy shouted. "It's in the closet."

"Well, get your fat ass over there and get it."

Rod walked to the closet. When he saw the standup wall safe, his eyes got big as saucers.

"Open it!" he joyfully said, touching the back of Andy's head with the gun.

After three nervous attempts, Andy opened the safe. He knew he could always get more money, so he stepped back and was forced to watch the robber take his hard-earned money.

"Get down on your knees," Rod said, pulling out the roll of tape. He wrapped Andy's mouth, hands and ankles, and then walked out of the office. When he made it to the front, Maine and Tony were pulling up. He walked out of the Finance Company and hopped in the car. "Drive!" he told Maine.

"I thought you was going in the movie gallery," Tony said with a bewilder look on his face.

"Yo, I changed my mind, son."

"What? You come all the way down here to try and get a loan?" Maine asked.

"The loan is official, son," Rod told them as he dumped the money on the front passenger floor of the car.

"What the fuck!" Maine exclaimed as he stared at all the money.

Tony looked over the seat at the money. He wasn't stupid. He knew Rod had just robbed the store, but he had to ask, "So you just robbed the spot?" Tony asked.

"You damn right, son. Fuck those wet-backs. They still owe us 40 acres and a mule."

Tony looked at the money again. It had taken Rod five minutes to come up. He thought about what all he could do with the money.

"So how much do we get?" Maine asked.

"Son, you know I ain't on no shady shit," Rod explained, knowing he had just turned these boys out.

Maine drove back to Tina's apartment to divide the money; he was already thinking about what he would do with his share. Tony sat in the back seat in a daze.

"Finally!" he mumbled to himself. He would be able to help his sister.

They pulled up at the apartment and went inside. Tina was on the sofa watching soap operas.

"What's up Tina?" Maine asked as he walked through the door.

"Hey yall," she responded without taking her eyes off the TV.

They walked to the back room. Rod dumped the money on Tony's bed, and then took a seat and watched them out of the corner of his eye. He wanted to see how thirsty they were.

"Let's count it!" Maine suggested, eyeing the money.

"I got this, yo," Rod told them as he counted the money. When he was done, they were all staring at $10,000 dollars. "Ok son, this your homie," Rod said passing Maine $2,500. Then he grabbed the other stack and gave it to Tony. "Yo, this yours."

As the two continued to watch, Rod took the rest of the money and stuffed it in his pockets. "What?" he asked, hunching his shoulders.

"Why didn't we split it fifty-fifty?" Tony asked.

"Yo, it's my lick, son. You want half, then you lace the joint, and I'll ride with you on it."

Tony thought about what Rod said and knew he was right. Hell, he didn't even know what was going on. "That's what's up. Give me a second," he said as he opened his room door to let them out. Tony took $500 from his stack and placed the rest under his bed inside a shoe box from the last pair of Jordan's he bought. The shoes were long worn out, so the first thing on his agenda was to get a new pair. He walked out of the bedroom and looked over at his sister. She was in the same spot. Glued to the TV, "Tina," he called out.

"What Tony? I don't want to miss this part," she said.

Tony walked over to her and handed her two hundred dollars.

"Here, go get some food and buy my nephew a toy or something."

"Where did you get this money, Tony?"

"You want it or not?" he asked as he reached back for it.

"Yeah, but..." Tina said, pulling the money out of his reach.

"Well, stop asking questions. We're bout to be straight," he stated as he walked out of the door.

When he got outside, Rod and Maine were waiting in the car. Tony hopped in and looked at Maine. "Let's hit the mall. I wanna can cop those new J's."

"Say no more!" Maine said as he pulled off.

Tony only brought enough money to buy the Jordan's and one outfit, but he was satisfied. This was the most money he'd ever had in his life, and he loved the feeling.

"Maine!" Tony called out as he walked into Foot Locker.

"What's up?" Maine asked, handing the cashier three crisp one-hundred-dollar bills.

"Would you like the socks too?" The cashier asked.

"Fuck it! Why not," he said as he gave Tony a pound. "I told you my cousin was like that."

"Yeah, he good, but what are we gonna do when he leaves?"

"Fool, we gonna keep getting money."

"How?" Tony asked confused.

"I got you. Just don't worry."

***

They headed out the mall.

"Rod, we hitting the club tonight?"

"Club 3DL - Maybe."

"What's up with us?" Maine asked.

"Nah, son. I don't do the crowds, plus I'm heading back up-state tomorrow."

"Bet that!" Maine stated as he bobbed his head to the music.

"Welcome to McDonalds. May I take your order, please," Mindy said through the headset.

Mindy was working the drive-thru and the line was around the building. She hated working the window. Not only did it stay busy, but every nigga that came through tried to get her number. She knew all the lines by heart. "Is you on the menu with the desert? or Hold the sugar please and just stick your finger in it. And the most common. I'm looking at the best McDonald's has to offer, so I guess I'll have to settle for seconds," she hummed them all to herself as she looked at the clock. Her lunch break was in five more minutes. "Welcome to McDonald's may I take your order?" she asked the next customer.

"Yeah, let me get...What y'all niggas want?" the voice stated pausing to get orders. Mindy's heart began to pound. She knew that voice anywhere.

She tried to look at the vehicle, but it was still around the corner.

"Yeah... yeah, let me get two number threes. No fucking onions and two number sixes all the way. Super-size the drinks, three cokes and a sweet tea."

"$21.70, drive around, please." Mindy watched as the black Camaro pulled up to the pick-up window. When she opened the glass, she was face to face with Tweet. He was picking through bills in his console, trying to find a small bill.

"All I got is hundreds," Tweet stated. "I got you, don't worry."

He looked around, as he extended the money and was surprised at who he saw. "Oh, what's up Mindy?" he asked as he started waving the money at her.

"Nothing much," she replied as she took the money and begin to count out his change. Mindy handed the bags to Tweet. She placed the drinks in a paper cup holder and begin to count out his change.

"Here's your change..." she reached out the window

"I don't do change!" Tweet told her, cutting her off. "So when are you gonna let me take you out? Kinda make up for last night."

"Look at my arm," Mindy complained, showing him the bruise.

"I'm sorry, bae. A nigga was fucked up. Let a nigga make it up to you."

Mindy threw the money in Tweet's car, making sure it fell on the floor. She looked at him with a disgusted look. "Just stay away from me!" she snapped before slamming the window.

"Bitch!" Tweet shouted as he pulled off.

* * * *

Tweet dropped his crew off and headed home. He pumped up the radio as he passed a crowd of onlookers. He mashed the gas and the Camaro launched forward, allowing him to make it home in no time.

He pulled up to the electric gate, and as he continued to eat his sandwich, the gate slowly opened.

"Preciate it," he yelled at the guard, right as he drove through.

After he parked, he walked into the living room to find his

father sitting in his lazy boy. He was facing a huge window that overlooked his swimming pool, guest house and golf course.

When L.G. heard his son walk in, he raised up out the chair to face him. "What did I ask you to do last night?"

L.G. was getting ready to retire from the game. He had survived the streets for twenty years. The game had been good to him and now he was stepping down. He wanted to crown his son as the new king, but he knew there was a lot of work to be done. He had tried to mold him after his image, and he wanted him to be a man about his business.

"Son, in order for these streets to respect you, you have to give them something to respect," he stated with a serious expression on his face.

"Oh Pop. I'm about to take care of that right now," Tweet said, knowing he fucked up big time.

L.G. stormed over and jacked Tweet up against the wall, causing his drink to fall on the expensive rug. Mutha' fucka, you listen to me. I got a million-dollar operation that's been feeding your black ass all your life. All I asked you to do was go around and pick up the money, and you can't do that. This is your last chance. If you're not man enough to run this operation, I guarantee you these streets gonna eat yo' ass alive. Now get the fuck outta my face," he growled as he let him down and pushed him away.

L.G. watched as his son walked away. He had his bodyguard follow him last night. After finding out Maurice went to the club; he sent another driver to pick up his money. This was it. If Maurice couldn't handle the operation, then he would not hold his hand. In this game only the strong survived.

CHAPTER THREE

"BLOOD ON MY HAND"

It had been three months since Rod taught Tony and Maine the stick-up game. Tony sat in his room counting the money from last night's lick. It was too sweet. Him and Maine had walked into, 'The Cool Spot', a bar that closed at midnight during the weekdays.

"We are closed, mon," the Haitian said, pointing at the clock. "Yeah, I know. I just got to use your restroom right quick," Tony said, walking towards the restroom to prevent the Haitian from rejecting him. As he made his way towards the back, he looked around the bar, and then texted Maine, who was waiting in the car.

Tony: Clear... one behind the counter
Maine: Count down from 15 and walk out.

Tony stood in the mirror as he counted backwards in his head. When he made it to three, he pulled the pistol from his waist, then pulled the ski mask over his face and walked out. When Tony made it to the counter, he paused. "What the fuck!" he exclaimed, as he looked around for Maine and the Haitian. He made his way behind the counter and paused. "Mmmmmmmmmmm....mmmm."

Tony opened the door that read 'Staff Only'. Once inside, he saw that his childhood friend had turned into a seasoned killer. Maine had the Haitian naked, tied up and lying on the floor. Tony could see blood spurt from the cuts, as Maine pulled the box cutter across his thighs. "Where the fuck is the money!" He snapped.

"Me no have nothing, mon."

"This mother fucka thinks he's tough," Maine said, looking back at Tony.

"Step back!" Tony ordered.

Tony pulled a Bic lighter out of his pocket. He walked up to the Haitian and got down on one knee. "When they get tough, you gotta get tougher."

Tony grabbed the Haitian's limp dick with his bare hand.

He struck the lighter to create a flame that lit up the entire room. "Say goodbye to your little friend," he told him in his best Scarface voice. Tony placed the flame on the Haitian's dick, and he screamed out in pain.

"Ohhhhhh, shit... mon! I talk. I talk! Please mon, no more fire to me dick," he pleaded.

"Where's the money?" Tony asked with the flame still glowing. He hoped the mutha' fucka hurried, because the lighter was getting hot and low on fumes. "Next time that mutha' fucka coming off."

"Da floor... on the floor, mon... Da money is in the floor."

"Point mutha' fucka!" Tony snapped.

The Haitian slowly pointed to the corner of the room. "Move da cabinet."

Maine walked to the cabinet and pushed it to the far wall. He saw a small rope attached to a screw. He pulled the rope, and the trap door swung open, "Bingo!" He said looking at Tony.

Maine pulled a black bag out of his pocket and began to fill it with money. Maine felt something else at the bottom of the safe.

He pulled the items out and discovered two kilos of cocaine.

"Check this out," he said to Tony. "Put it in the bag and let's dip."

They walked out the bar to Maine's car. Tony thought about the fact that the Haitian saw his face when he first walked in.

"Wait for me in the car," Tony told Maine as he turned on his heels and headed back into the bar.

Tony knew what he had to do. Kill the Haitian. He had never taken a life before. So far, they had been successful with just showing their victims the pistol. He begun to sweat as the hairs rose on his neck. He walked back in the office, and the Haitian was still on the floor.

"There's nuttin more, mon," he said as he looked up at Tony with fear in his eyes.

Tony raised the gun and took a deep breath. As Tony released his breath, he squeezed the trigger. He jumped as half of the Haitians face left his body. Tony closed his eyes and whispered, "A dead man can't talk or seek revenge."

When he made it to the car, Maine was waiting with the engine running. "What did you forget my G?" he asked when Tony hopped in.

"I had to destroy any evidence," he replied.

* * * *

Mindy walked into the house to find her mother sitting at the table with a confused look on her face.

"Come here, Mindy," she said in a sharp tone.

"What's up?" Mindy asked as she walked over to her mother.

Sarah looked over her body as if she was looking for something.

She grabbed Mindy's arm, causing her to jump from the pain. "I'm only gonna ask you one time. What happened to your arm?"

Mindy stared at her mother. She knew her well enough to know that when she asked a question that direct, she already knew the answer. She thought about telling a lie but knew that would only make things worse.

"I was at the club the other night with Meka and this guy was drunk..."

"Who!" She asked, cutting her off. "Mama, it's not that serious."

"Look at your damn arm!" She shouted. "Have you seen the bruises on it? Who did this to you?"

Mindy had seen it and had been taking ibuprofen to ease the pain. She didn't want to blow things out of proportion, but her mother was not letting it go.

"Tweet," she finally mumbled.

"Tweet! Who the hell is, Tweet? What's his name Mindy?"

"Maurice Goines."

Sarah looked at her daughter with a look of disbelief. She stood up and walked over to her daughter, placing her hands on her cheeks, she held her face steady. "Listen to me, Mindy. Stay as far away from him as you can. Do you understand me?"

"Yes Ma'am!"

"No... don't just hear me. Do it! Are we clear?"

"I hear you, Mama. He just keeps tryna go out with me. I've told him no, over and over. He's just stupid."

As Sarah listened to her daughter. She thought about her own childhood, when her mother didn't protect her, as her mother's instincts kicked in, she could only say, "I love you, and I'll always protect you."

She left the room and went into her bedroom and closed the door behind her.

Mindy watched as her mother walked away. She couldn't understand what the big deal was all about, so she dismissed the thought and headed to her bedroom. Her phone went off as she laid across the bed. She looked at the screen and saw that it was Meka.

"Hey ho!" she answered.

"What's up, bitch," Meka followed up.

"Nothing! I just walked in the house. Girl, let me tell you what happened."

Mindy gave Meka the rundown of how her mother acted out about her bruises. She told her how her mother had demanded that she stay away from Tweet.

"Damn, she must know you still got new pussy," Meka joked.

"So what! It's better than that loose pussy you got," she said as they both burst out laughing.

Mindy didn't mind Meka joking with her about her virginity. She'd never gone all the way, and the closest she had ever been to having sex, was a kiss. When sex was their subject on conversation, she generally listened at Meka talk about her and Zack's sex life. On one occasion, she'd ended a call with her friend, and her phone suddenly rang back with Meka's ringtone. When Mindy answered the phone, she could hear Meka screaming passionately as Zack sexed her down. Being nosey, she kept the phone to her ear, and before she knew it, she had her hands in her panties. She began to rub her clit back and forth, and then she tried to insert her finger inside her pussy, but the pain was too intense. As Meka screamed louder, she could hear Zack's voice.

"Whose pussy is this?"

"It's your!" Meka screamed from the pleasure.

Mindy closed her eyes and pictured Zack fucking her. She opened her legs wider, as her tight pussy got wetter. She felt a sensation building, as her first orgasm began to form, when Meka screamed out that she was cumming. Mindy felt the flow of hot fluid on her hands. She hung up the phone and fell into a daze. If this is what sex felt like, she couldn't wait to try it.

* * * *

Tweet sat at the round table with his father. Today his father would let all the Trap Bosses know that he would be stepping down. He would hand the streets over to his son. L.G. had also arranged a meeting with the Cartel to let them know he was passing the torch. Tweet looked around at the guys at the table. He couldn't wait until his father got out the way. He watched as his father sipped on a glass of wine at the head of the table.

"Take this seat, son," he said, pointing at the chair.

Tweet took the seat at the head of the table. Immediately, his father explained to his long-time crew that he was stepping down. They would no longer report to him.

"So how we get resupplied?" Oak, one of L.G.'s trusted bosses asked.

"My son will take care of all that," L.G. assured.

Oak looked at Tweet. He knew that the kid was not about his business like L.G. Oak had even asked L.G. to let him oversee the operation. But L.G.'s mind was made up. He wanted his son in charge. He knew that Tweet like to party and chase Ho's, which was a toxic combination that just didn't mix with business.

"Who will pick up the money?" Tess asked.

Tess was L.G.'s accountant. She counted all the money from the Trap spots as soon as it was turned in. She had been with L.G. over ten years. The only person who had more time in the organization than her was Oak. But that didn't matter, because she gave L.G.

something Oak never could – Good pussy. L.G. looked at each member of his team.

"My son will take care of business. Ain't that right, son?" he asked, directing his attention to Tweet.

"I got this. Everybody just keep the money coming, and we gonna be just fine."

The crew looked at Tweet with a look of disbelief. Only a new jack would say some shit like that. But they would just have to break him in.

"Yall excuse him," L.G. cut in. "Just give him time. He'll get it together."

Tweet looked around the room. He didn't have a clue what they were talking about.

"The meeting is over. You all may leave. It's been a joy working with each of you."

As the crew filed out of the room, L.G. watched as Maurice hurried to leave.

"Son!" he called out.

Tweet turned around. He was hoping to get out before he was stopped. He had shit to do. He watched as Tess walked up to L.G. and whispered something in his ear. Tess had a fat ass. She always dressed like a business lady, but you could tell she was holding. As soon as Tweet was in full command, his first order for her would be to let him hit that.

"What's up pop?" he asked, standing.

"Listen, the first thing you gotta learn is you and every member of your crew is a team. It's not about you. It's not about the money. And it's not about pussy," he said, letting him know he caught his son's eyes on Tweet's ass. "You gotta make them feel like they are appreciated. I will not hold your hand through this; nor will I correct your mistakes. In this game, you will either drown or swim. The choice is yours. Oh, and before I forget, leave Mindy alone."

"I go it, Pops," Tweet said as he turned and walked out puzzled by his father's orders.

L.G. watched as his son left the room. He had been in this game a long time, and he could spot a true hustler a mile away. Something told him that his son had a lot of growing up to do.

* * * *

"Six thousand a piece," Tony said as he split the money from the Haitian with Maine.

"So what we gonna do with the work?" Maine asked. Not only did Tony and Maine hit for twelve-grand, but the Haitian had two kilos of coke in the stash. "How much do you think it's worth?" Maine asked.

"I don't know, but I know who we can ask," Tony said, picking up his phone to call his sister. "Tina."

"Hey! What's up?"

"Where you at?"

"Home, why?" she replied in a concerned manner.

"What's Flea's number?"

Flea was Tina's baby daddy and a small-time hustler. He was a good dude and Tony knew he could trust him. Even though he would never sell drugs, money was money, and he would let Flea sell the drugs, and just break him off.

"I gotta get a driver's license," Tony said.

"That ain't shit. I'll take you tomorrow, my G."

"That's what's up," Tony said, looking at the number his sister texted him. "Okay, I'll holla back," he said, hanging up to call Flea.

"Who this!" Flea answered.

"This Tony. Where you at?"

"Tony, what's up bra-law? A nigga out here grinding. What's

the deal?"

"Meet me at the crib, asap," Tony said before hanging up.

Tony knew he wanted to be big time, so he decided to let him do all the talking, just to see where he was at. When they pulled up, Flea was on the side of the apartment serving a crack-head. Tony hopped out of the car and walked up to him.

"Don't ever let me see you do that shit where I lay my head. The next time, we won't have this conversation," he expressed.

"My bad homie," Flea said, aware of the fact that he'd fucked up. They walked to the back room and Flea stood nervously watching the two. "What up? Why you call me over here?" he asked as he looked from one to the other. Tony pulled one of the kilos out the backpack and threw it on the bed. When Flea saw the cocaine, his eyes bulged. "Fuck! You gotta whole brick," he said, looking at Tony.

"You want to buy it?" Tony asked.

"Shit! I ain't gonna lie. I ain't got it like that, but I know who might want it. What's the ticket?"

"What do they go for?"

"Right now, with the drought, thirty-three easy."

"I tell you what. Sell it for thirty-three and keep two-grand for yourself," Tony said as he gave Flea the kilo.

"That's love," Flea said as he stuffed the kilo inside his shirt.

"I got another one," Tony said.

"Say no more, I'll be back," Flea said as he walked out.

* * * *

L.G. paced back and forth in his office on his cell phone. "What do you mean you need more money? I send you money every month. As a matter of fact, I've been sending yo ass money for eighteen years," he screamed into the phone.

As he listened, he looked out his office door to make sure no one could overhear his conversation.

"You listen to me, bitch! If you ever threaten me again, you won't ever get another penny from me. Do you understand?" he snapped, ending the call.

He walked to his bar, filled his glass with vodka, gulped down the entire glass, and then refilled it.

"Somebody's having a bad day," Tess teased as she walked out of her office.

L.G. jumped and turned around. "I didn't know you was still here," he shockingly said.

"Well, I was supposed to leave two hours ago, but Maurice forgot to make the rounds and pick up the money. Oak did the pick-up and brought it to me. I just finished packaging it up to be shipped out."

"That damn boy!"

"Well, I guess it's like you said, we're just gonna have to work with him."

L.G. looked at Tess. Her long black hair fell across her slim shoulders. She never wore tight fitting clothes, leaving her figure to the imagination. L.G. knew her well though, since he'd been fucking Tess for years. He walked over to her and placed his lips on her mouth. She opened it and let him in. He opened her blouse and freed her breast from their 36DD cups.

"Ahhh!" She moaned as he rubbed her fingers across her nipples.

L.G. picked her up and sat her on his desk. He ran his hands up her skirt and felt her warm mound inside her panties. He raised her skirt to her waist and pulled her panties to one side. Lowering his head L.G. slowly let his tongue part Tess's pussy lips and worked his tongue in and out of her moist pussy. Tess pushed her hips forward, grinding on his face. She felt her orgasm building as he pushed his hot tongue deep inside her tight vagina.

"Right... there, right there!" She begged for dear life.

When she couldn't hold it any longer, she closed her thighs against his head. "I'm Cumming!" She screamed out in a long moan. L.G. continued to lap her juices as they ran down her thighs. He stood up and Tess unbuckled his pants. "Fuck me daddy!" She begged.

L.G. pulled his dick out and shoved it inside her warm tight walls. Her wetness allowed him to slide in with ease. He began to stroke her pussy while she matched him stroke for stroke. As he pushed deeper, she tightened her muscles around his dick.

"Yes...Daaaddddyyy! "She screamed as he fucked her long and hard. "It feels so good, don't stop."

L.G. loved how Tess's pussy felt. He felt his nut building and picked up his pace. He was stroking deep inside her, and she was throwing that pussy back just how he liked it. L.G.'s nuts became tight, as the wet slapping sound took him over the edge.

"Aaahhh!" He growled.

Tess placed her hand around his waist and pulled him as far into her as she could. When their juices mixed, he was deep inside of her. They stayed that way for a moment, as both enjoyed the feeling of the other.

"That was so good, daddy. Take all that stress out on this pussy," she panted.

L.G. felt his dick stiffen again. Tess began to roll her hips from the hardness. As he began to stroke her again, she closed her eyes. She knew this go around would be a challenge. She squeezed her eyes closed as he pushed deep inside her pussy.

Spreading her legs as wide as possible, she lost herself to the pain and pleasure of his strokes.

It was two hours later when Tess walked out of L.G.'s office. She was sore from the fucking he had just put on her. For the two, there were times when he made love to her, and during other intimate times, he'd fucked the shit out of her. With the pain she felt between her thighs, love was nowhere in the picture.

As Tess walked to her car, she met Tweet on the driveway. "Hey, I need to holla at you."

"What's up?" she asked.

"Well, I was wondering if you wanted to be my personal assistant."

"What do you mean?" she asked, wanting to make sure she'd heard him right.

"You know... personal assistant. A few things I might need that you can provide," he said, looking her body up and down.

Tess looked at Tweet with a stupid look. If he only knew that she could barely walk right now from the fucking his daddy had just put on her, he would probably shit. Instead of killing his ego, she decided to just lay the baby down easily.

"Listen, the number one thing you gotta learn is to control your small head. You gonna get enough pussy that you won't have a need for mines, ok? It's not good to mix feelings with money. It's the quickest way to create problems."

"Well, if you change your mind. The offer still stands," he said as he walked off.

As Tess pulled out of the driveway, she glanced back at Tweet through her rearview mirror. "I don't do boys; I do real men!" She stated, then mashed the gas a little for emphasis.

CHAPTER FOUR

"RIDING FLY"

Tony stood at the dealership staring at the rows of cars. Maine had taken him to the DMV (Department of Motor Vehicles) to get his license. He walked past a black BMW 650 Coupe. *Too flashy,* he thought to himself.

He continued to walk through the cars when he noticed the white car parked on the advertisement rack. Tony walked up to the car and read the tag. 2015 Audi SS Coupe, 0-60 mph in 3.7 seconds, all leather and fully loaded.

"If you're buying today, I can replace the 18-inch factory rims with a set of 30's," a voice said from behind him. "Just got her in yesterday." Tony looked around at the bushy haired white man. He was swinging the keys to the car as he continued to talk. "If you like, we can do the rims off-set. I was thinking Ashanti's with a white back drop. You do know it carries a 1,000-watt sound system. It's the perfect car, not too flashy, but makes a hell of a statement"

"How much?" Tony asked.

"Thirty-eight five," the salesman said as he started counting his commission in his head.

Tony had been around, so he knew how to bargain. he looked at the guy and pulled out a stack of money. "30,000 cash!"

"I can't sell her for that."

"Well let me talk to the person that can. I got $30,000 to spend. Take it or I'm walking."

"Thirty-five, and that's rock bottom," the salesman said, watching his commission go down the drain.

"Thirty-two... final offer."

The salesman looked around at the building. He could see his co-workers waiting on him to lose the sale, so they could step in and make it. Not wanting to look like a failure, he turned his attention back to Tony. "Sir, let's get the paperwork done. By the way, my name is Jeff," he said as he gave Tony a firm handshake. "Follow me to my office."

* * * *

Two hours later, Tony pulled up in front of the apartment.

Flea was sitting on the porch smoking a blunt. Tony hopped out the new ride and walked to the porch.

"I see you doing big things," Elea said, looking past him at the car.

"Just a little sumptin, sumptin to get me off the pavement."

"I got that money for you. Plus, my dude wants to cop the other one," Flea said as he followed Tony into the apartment.

"Call him!"

Flea counted out the money as he talked on the phone. When he was done, he turned to Tony. "It's all good."

"Bet that," Tony said as he past him the last kilo. Flea walked out of the house, leaving Tony to his thoughts.

Tony's life had taken a complete turn. He had gone from poor and hungry to more money than he could spend. As he stuffed the money into his burglar proof wall safe, he walked into the bathroom, stripped down and stepped into the shower.

Tony let the hot water pounce up again his body, relaxing his muscles. He didn't understand what was happening to him. He had money now, but still watched every corner for a weak victim. He changed his thoughts to the Fall Festival that was going down this weekend at 3DL. This was his coming out party. The city was about to learn that he was on top of his game. Maine had already booked the V.I.P. The thought of balling with the elite caused a smile to spread across his face. Tony walked to the living room to find Tina glued to the TV as usual.

"Damn, you love those soap operas," he said to her.

"Boy, Victor Newman just found out Jack fucked Nikki."

"Whatever," he said, paying her no mind. "Listen, when Flea brings back that money, take a rack and stash the rest."

"Okay!" Tina said without blinking from the TV.

Tony walked outside to call Maine.

"What's up, my G?" Maine asked.

"What the duck look like?" Tony asked.

"Sitting pretty!"

"Three o'clock."

"Perfect timing," Maine said before ending the call.

Tony and Maine had a lick set up for tonight. It wasn't the normal lick, but all the businesses were hot. Right now, they really didn't need the money, but Maine said it was too sweet to pass up.

* * * *

Mindy walked through the mall singing the tunes to Drake's latest number one hit, *'Hot Line Bling'*. She had just bought an outfit for the Fall Festival. Once again, Meka had talked her into going.

Ever since she had heard Zack fucking Meka, she had been having feelings between her legs. It was like a small itch that needed scratching. Mindy walked into The Stagg Shop to do some window shopping, unless she spotted something that beat out what she already had purchased.

The store catered to men, but a sister could find some fly shit in here too. She walked around the store picking up outfits only to put them back. She turned to head out of the store, but stopped in her tracks when she noticed a manikin wearing a black Gucci body dress made for her. The back was open, and it had diamond studded shoulder straps. She walked up to the dress, looked at the $999.00 price tag and shook her head. Clearly, it was almost her whole month's paycheck.

"I bet that dress would look good on you," a voice said, causing her to jump.

She turned around and was face to face with Tony. Mindy hadn't seen Tony since that night at the club when Tweet pulled her arm. He had stepped in to help her, and she hadn't been able to thank him. He was dressed fly as hell today. His hair cut was fresh making him handsome in his own way. Mindy noticed that itch started down between her legs. To break the stare, she turned back to the dress.

"Hello Tony. It is nice, but they probably don't have my size."

"Of course, they do. Excuse me!" he called out to the sale's assistant.

"Tony wait..." Mindy pleaded, knowing she couldn't afford the dress.

"May I help you?" The sales lady asked.

"No!" Mindy interjected.

"Yes!" Tony said, cutting her off. "Take her to the dressing room and fit her for this dress for me please."

"But Tony..."

"Go Mindy!" He commanded.

Mindy walked off with the lady. As she tried on different dresses, she noticed that the itch between her legs had turned into a small thump. When she found the perfect size, she walked out so that Tony could see it.

"You're beautiful!" Tony exclaimed.

"Thank you, but I don't have the money to buy this."

"And I didn't ask you if you had the money, did I?" he asked her as he gave her a demanding stare. "Take this dress and put it with the stuff I have at the counter," he told the sales assistant.

"Tony, you don't have to do this," Mindy whispered. "Go change. I'll meet you at the cashier counter," he said as he walked off.

They met at the counter, and Tony paid for their outfits. As they walked out of the store, he looked over at her. "You hungry? I know this quiet Italian restaurant."

"Sure," Mindy said without thinking.

They made it to the restaurant and Mindy was surprised when Tony didn't have to wait. The waiter noticed him and immediately walked them to a private booth. They ordered their food and sipped wine while they waited for the food to arrive.

Tony was funny with a serious edge. She had always seen him as family, but that image had changed. Mindy didn't know what it was, but Tony had her full attention. And the way he practically made her put on the dress, had her panties wet.

They laughed so much, as they enjoyed a great dinner. He would occasionally make jokes at people passing by, and they would cry with laughter. When their meal was finished, he left a one-hundred-dollar bill on the table.

"I really had a great time, Tony," she honestly stated.

"That's what' s up. That dress is for our second date."

"Oh yeah! And when will that be?"

"This weekend. The Fall Festival."

"I'm supposed to be going with Meka," she disappointingly said.

"Well, that's cool. I'll be there in the V.I.P. section, just walk to the V.I.P. window and tell'em you're with me. Section four."

"Ok thanks again," she said, standing to exit.

They walked out of the restaurant, and he followed her to her car.

"Where did you park?" she asked him.

"Right there," he said, pointing at his ride.

"It's nice."

"It's alright... Look I gotta get going. Friday night, right?"

"Friday night," Mindy said with a smile on her face.

* * * *

Tweet sat at the head of the table as he stared at the overall report. Everything was down. The movement of the product, the money, and not to mention, one of their trap houses had been busted by the cops. He looked up at the crew.

"What the fuck happened?" he snapped.

"Whoa... youngblood!" Oak snapped back. "Easy with the temper."

"What the fuck do you mean? We done lost over a million dollars in one week. And you telling me to be easy," Tweet snapped back.

"Listen, we lost the money, but we can make it back," one of the trap bosses spoke up.

"This shit ain't gonna fly. I'm not gonna be soft like my daddy when mutha' fuckas fuck up. They gotta pay," Tweet snapped again.

"What the hell is all the yelling about?" Tess asked as she walked out of her office.

"This ain't yo business!" Tweet turned on her.

"Excuse me!"

"You heard me. I done lost too much fucking money."

"Well, it's about damn time you start paying attention. You running around here like you don't give a shit about this operation. I don't know if anybody told you, but this shit don't run itself," Tess fumed. "These people work for you. If you can't sit your ass down and take care of business, then you can look for a lot more money not being made," she continued.

"I don't need you trying to tell me shit."

"Fine, but don't say I didn't warn you; especially when this whole operation blows up in your fucking face," she said, storming out.

Tweet turned around to find everybody leaving except Oak. "Where the hell are yall going?" he asked, but nobody answered. "I didn't dismiss yall," he yelled as the trap bosses continued to walk out, as if they didn't hear him talking. Oak just watched and shook his head. He knew this kid had a lot to learn. "Hey! Get back in here now!" Tweet shouted, as the last person walked out leaving him and Oak alone. Tweet walked around the office full of anger. He looked out the window and watched as his trap bosses drove off. "Fuck! he shouted. "Fuck...fuck...fuck!" he continued, kicking over a chair.

Oak watched in silence, as the young buck lost his cool. He waited for him to calm down before saying anything.

"Have a seat at the head of the table," Oak told him.

"For what? It's a little too late for that, ain't it?"

"Look, you gotta learn to stay in control. No matter what happens, your crew must always believe in you. You've lost the trust of your workers, and that's a bad thing," Oak told him, as he walked towards him. "The first thing you gotta do is let your team know that you got their back at all times. You don't have to throw it in their faces that you're the boss, and you owe Tess an apology. She works her ass off, and she didn't deserve to be talked to that way. Next, you need to send everybody an apology with the request to have another meeting. These drugs don't sell themselves, as much as you may not want to admit it, you need every one of them – just like they need you."

"But..." was all Tweet got out before Oak took control of the conversation.

"I promised your pops that I'd have your back, but you must be willing to let me help you," Oak advised when Tweet tried to cut him off. "That's your problem, you want to talk, but don't know what you're talking about. So let me finish. There's money to be made, son. Let's get on the right path and make it," Oak had had enough, so he walked out as well.

Tweet knew the old man was right, but they needed to understand that the operation had a new boss, and it would run his way. If they couldn't accept that, then he would find new bosses. He got up and headed out of the office. As he passed Tess's office, he thought about how fat her ass was when she walked away.

"The offer still stands," he said as he exited.

"Fuck you!" she shouted.

* * * *

Tony was riding down Main Street after leaving Mindy. He glanced at the two old men unloading money from a Wells Fargo truck. He immediately picked up his cell phone and called Maine.

"What's up, my G?" Maine answered.

"Yo, what's your cousin Rod's number?"

"516-243-0859. Why? What's up?"

"I want to ask him something. I got a little lick I'm looking at."

"What you need him for, we got the gift of gab now."

"Just let me handle this, bra," Tony told him, then ended the call.

"Yo son, who is dis?" Rod answered as he checked the area code of the call.

"This Tony's man. What's up?"

"I hear ya'll shaking up that little county, that's what's up."

"We doing a little something. But hey, I want to ask you something about the bank bags. How do you know which one has the dye packs, and which ones are official?"

"Oh, shit son! Y'all little niggas stepping it up now. It's easy. Just don't fuck with the ones with the red serial numbers. Red is dead."

"I gotcha, preciate the look out."

"Anytime, son," Rod said, ending the call.

* * * *

Mindy was up early scrambling to get herself ready for work. She practically stayed up all night thinking about Tony. For some odd reason, the itch in her panties was at an all-time high every time he crossed her mind. She eventually fell asleep, but it took forever for her to come out of the dream she had throughout the night.

Her mind was trying to resurrect the way Tony manhandled her in her dream. As she walked past the television, the news reporter was live on the scene somewhere on Main Street. The story he was covering got her full attention.

"This is Darlene Hampton with a breaking story. A bank

on Main Street is the crime scene of a gruesome murder. Two Wells Fargo truck drivers were found shot to death, and an undisclosed amount of money is missing from the truck. Police are on the scene as we speak, looking for any possible clues as to who would do something this tragic. As of now, there are no witnesses, and no possible suspects. As the story unfolds, we will keep you updated. This is Darlene Hampton with Action News Nine. Back to you Tom."

The news went on describing the two men that was murdered as they did their job, but Mindy's mind drifted off. She wondered. *Who would do such a heinous act to those old men, they were somebody's father, grandfather, brother or son?* She felt their families pain, but all that came to an end when her mother came in the room with something else on her mind.

* * * *

Tony laid in his bed looking at the ceiling. He called himself counting the cracks in it, but lost count every time. He couldn't believe how his life had changed overnight, but he was loving his transition at the same time. Plus, he was this close to getting Mindy, the girl of his dreams.

He wondered if she thought of him the same way now that he had his paper up and was a nigga to be reckon with on the streets. He glanced over at the money he made a couple of hours earlier. He knew it was wrong to do what he had done to the old men, but a dead man can't talk, and he would have hated to give up his fame, when he had just become the leading actor. His phone rung on the nightstand, he looked at the caller ID, then smiled before answering it.

Maine had called to talk about another lick they could pull off tonight. Tony thought about objecting, but he was all about them dead presidents.

* * * *

Tony and Maine sat in the woods and watched the old warehouse. Maine said that one of L.G.'s workers moved work through it. They really didn't need the money, since the armor truck robbery put them ahead of the game, but a lick was a lick.

There was little movement and Tony was wondering if anybody was there. Finally, he saw the roll-up door rise, giving a clear view throughout the warehouse.

"I only see one person," Maine whispered.

"That's all I see. Let's move," Tony suggested as he began to walk towards the back of the warehouse.

Maine pointed towards a parked car as they split up. "It's empty, I already checked it," Tony told him.

They made their way to the back of the warehouse. It was dark, which was perfect for the mission. As Tony crawled to the front towards the rolled-up door, he could see Maine crawling towards the main entrance. Maine could see the person inside, so he waved for Tony to continue coming.

Tony raised off his stomach into the squat position. He slowly eased up and peeked over the ledge. He could see the guy talking away on his cell phone. Tony looked over at Maine and waved for him to go in. With his hands up, he counted down from five using hand signals.

Tony picked up a stone off the ground and tossed it against the wall to the right of the guy. With the phone still to his ear, he got up and walked towards the noise. Maine quickly ran behind him and placed the pistol to the back of his head.

"Tell her bye-bye," he whispered.

"Let me call you back," the guy said as he turned to face the ski-masked man and pistol.

Tony jumped into the warehouse and pulled down the roll-up door.

"Sit down," he ordered as he walked to the front door.

Tony locked the door and turned off the lights out front. He walked back over to Maine. As he wrapped tape around the guys legs, he looked into his eyes, for some reason Tony didn't see the fear that most of his victims had. He thought about the Haitian. A cold-blooded killer. Dismissing all other thoughts, he got down to the business at hand.

"Listen mutha' fucka! This can go two ways. You can tell me where the stash is and live, or you can die now, and we'll just search this mutha' fucka til we find it on our own," he said, knowing in the back of his mind that the guy was dead no matter what he decided.

"Yall niggas must don't know who the fuck I work for. If you know what's best for you, you'll walk out of here now, and hope I take this as a bad dream," the guy told them with a mug glued on his face.

"Have it your way then."

WHAM! sounded the pistol as he connected to the side of his head. "Let's play then," Tony directed him as he pointed to a corner of the warehouse.

He grabbed the guy and pulled his baggy pants and boxers down leaving him naked.

Rock had been robbed before, so if these two punks thought they could break a soldier; they were in for a rude awakening.

"Just go ahead and kill me, mutha' fucka. Before you do though suck this long, black dick," Rock said with an evil smirk on his face.

"I like this kind," Maine said as he pulled a pair of vise grip pliers from his back pocket and perfectly adjusted them. He walked over to Rock and clamped the grips across his shoe.

"Agggggh!!" Rock screamed as the bones in his toes cracked.

Maine stepped away, leaving the grips in place. Tony walked up and placed the straight razor against Rock's neck. Unphased, Rock begged him to kill him.

"Not yet!" Tony declared as he dropped the razor to his thigh, slashing through his skin like it was paper.

"Shit!" Rock screamed as he watched his blood leak out of the open wound.

Maine walked up and poured kerosene over Rock's whole body. "You got the light?" he asked Tony.

"No... no... no!" Rock pleaded.

"Time is running out," Tony said as he pulled out his Bic.

Rock knew that these guys were killers. They had the torture game down pack. This was his old life before meeting L.G. He knew that his death was close, and he needed to find a way to buy time or come out of this with his life after trying to play hard ball. He thought about the stash, and what L.G. would do to him. The last he'd heard, he was retired.

With that thought in mind, Rock pleaded for his life. "Okay, okay! I'll tell you what you wanna know, just don't kill me.

"Talk!" Tony said as he watched the two-inch flame dance before his eyes.

"It's in the basement," Rock screamed and nodded his head towards the door on the wall.

"Watch him!" Tony said as he walked towards the door. Tony opened the door and was blinded by the darkness.

He flicked the lighter, spotted the switch and turned it on. He walked down the staircase into the basement, looking around at the somewhat empty room. Seeing nothing worth taking, he turned to climb the steps when he spotted a huge wall safe underneath the stairs.

Tony walked around to find the safe cracked open. He pulled the door open and saw apple boxes stack at the bottom of the safe. Tony opened the first box and it was stuffed to the top with money. He could see more money through the top of the second box. Tony tried to lift it, but the extra weight made him wonder what was inside. he opened the box to find it only had a small layer of money across the top, underneath was stacks of kilos.

Tony took the bag out of his pocket and emptied both boxes, then tossed the bag over his shoulder and headed up the stairs. Maine still had Rock at gun point as he walked in their direction.

"What we got in the bag, Santa?" Maine jokingly asked.

"Lots of toys, now let's get outta here. Here take this," he instructed, passing Maine the bag.

Tony picked up the can of kerosene and began to splash it on the walls. He walked over to the basement door and splashed the stairs as well.

Rock looked at him cautiously. "You said you weren't gonna kill me!" Tony ignored him as he continued to douse the place with kerosene, until the big can was empty. He walked over to Rock who was still pleading for his life. "You said you weren't gonna kill me!" Rock repeated.

"I'm not!" Tony stated as he walked out of the building.

He stepped out of the side door, pulled a rag out of the trash can, lit it with his lighter and then tossed it back in the building into a puddle of kerosene. As the place went up in flames, he jogged around the corner where Maine was waiting, jumped in the car, and they pulled off.

* * * *

"Aaaw!" Tina screamed as Flea pounded deep inside her pussy

from behind. She pushed backwards, matching his strokes.

"Fuck me ...fuck me!" she screamed.

Flea continued to pound the walls of her pussy, as Tina reached between her legs and rubbed his balls. "Whose pussy is this?" he asked.

"It's yours, daddy. Don't stop... please... don't... aaaw!" Tina screamed as she released another orgasm.

Her body was drained. Exhausted, she fell forward on her face, causing him to slip out of her.

"Wait baby. Damn! I'm bout to nut," Flea stated, leaning forward to slide back inside of her tight warm walls. Once inside, he began to stroke her fast, to regain his near orgasm.

"Aaaaw!" Tina moaned, as she began to find her pace to match his. When she was nearing another orgasm, she felt his body as it began to jerk. Tina arched her back, giving Flea full access to her wet pussy.

"I'm cumming!" he grunted as he pushed as deep as he could. As she continued to roll her hips, he laid next to her exhausted. "Damn baby! You got some good pussy. I'mma fuck around and put another baby in you."

"You better not," Tina said as she continued to roll her hips against his still semi-hard dick.

"Hey!" a voice shouted from the other side of the door. Flea jumped up and grabbed his pistol. As he walked to the door, he snatched it open with his pistol pointed. "Get that shit out my face before you piss me off," Tony said as he looked past Flea at his sister.

"Why the fuck you yelling outside my door like that?" she asked him.

"Fuck that! Let me holla at'cha," he said to Flea before he turned and walked away.

"Give me a minute. Let me slide on my shit."

The Lick

As Flea got dressed, Tony put up his part of the money. The split was 100 grand each, plus the ten kilos of cocaine. Flea walked in the room still holding his gun.

"What's up Bra-law? Everything good?" he asked.

"Yeah, it's good. I got some more of those thangs."

"Damn!" Flea said amazed.

"This the deal, I'm gonna let you work all ten. Just give the money to Tina as you finish."

"That's what' s up."

"Tell her to get dressed. I got a surprise for her."

"Bet!" Flea said as he began to leave.

"Flea!"

"Yeah," he said, turning back to face Tony.

"I got the V.I.P. at 3DL, Fall Festival Night, Section Four. Be there."

"You know I will, bossman," Flea replied as he took off up the hallway.

CHAPTER FIVE

"THE ROOF IS ON FIRE"

L.G. sat in Tess's office with his arms folded. He was waiting on his son to call the meeting to order. Not only had the operation lost over two-million dollars in the last month, but Rock had gotten burned up in the warehouse the night before.

"You okay, daddy?" Tess asked, seeing the frustration on his face.

"I can't believe this shit!"

"He's not responsible. All he thinks about is partying and pussy."

"Hell, daddy he's even been trying to fuck me," she said to try and calm him.

The only thing that was on L.G.'s mind was the loss of his money. He listened as his son took the seat at the head of the table.

"Can anybody tell me what happened last night?" Tweet asked.

"Well, we lost a member of our team," Oak responded.

"How did they get into the warehouse?"

"I don't know that, but it's burned to the ground."

"How much product did we have?"

"I dropped off twenty kilos, two days ago. I called you yesterday to go by and pick up the 200 grand, but Tess said it's not accounted for, so we lost that as well."

Tweet got up and walked around the table. *Oh fuck!* he thought to himself. He was at the hotel with this fine ass bitch when Oak called him to pick up the money. The only person who knew that the money wasn't picked up was Tess. *Hopefully she ain't said shit to Pops yet.*

After the meeting, he would apologize to her for his rude behavior and ask her to sweep this one under the rug. He turned to face the trap bosses without a clue as to what to say, much less do.

"What we're gonna do is keep the operation going like normal," Tweet was saying until Oak cut him off.

"Are you fucking kidding me!" Oak snapped as he slammed his fist against the table.

At a loss for words, he looked over at Oak and shouted, "Well what the fuck do you suggest!"

"I suggest you sit yo god damn ass down. Now!" a voice shouted from behind them.

Oak smiled as he watched his longtime partner and friend walk to the table. He knew his friend well enough to know that he wouldn't sit back at a time like this in silence.

"Maurice! Son, you lost over a million dollars last night, and you tell the crew to keep operating like they normally do. Are you fucking stupid! The first order of business is to find out who hit that warehouse," L.G. tried reasoning with his son.

"School him Old G!" Oak spoke up.

L.G. stepped around his son to face the table. "I want ears to the streets," he said as he looked at every face in the room.

"Every fucking trap that ain't ours. We're going in. If you see a mutha' fucka with a gram of our work, I want to know who sold it to 'em. If they got a problem talking, take 'em to the dungeon, and I'll meet you there."

L.G. knew that the cocaine would be easy to locate. His last shipment was oil-based. A distinctive type of cocaine that carried a goldish brown tint, plus the logo on the kilos was stamped L.G.O.

"Oak!" he calmly stated.

"Yeah boss!" Oak replied, looking at Tweet as if he had just gotten demoted.

"I want you to hit the Scottsville area. I heard some young nigga over there was moving work."

"Got it boss."

Tweet watched his father as he gave all the Trap Bosses instructions. They left the room to go fulfill their loyalty. When L.G. was done talking, everybody was gone except his son.

He walked around the room in silence before he walked over to face him. Tweet braced himself, thinking a blow was about to come.

"Tess!" L.G. called out.

"Yes," Tess answered as she walked to the office door and stopped.

"Come over here!"

Tweet watched as her black mini skirt gripped her fat ass. When she walked by him, he didn't know what his father was up to, *unless this bitch done told him about the money already*. He prepared a lie in his mind, as his father and Tess stared at him like he was a total stranger.

"You like this!" L.G. stated as he grabbed Tess's skirt and pulled it up, revealing a pair of black laced thongs. "Is this why my operation just lost over two million dollars? Pussy!" He shouted through gritted teeth, still holding the skirt up.

Tess was embarrassed, but too terrified to move. She stood and watched as Tweet lustfully stared between her legs.

"It's not about that! Tweet mumbled."

"Then what the fuck is it about?" L.G. snapped as he lunged

towards him.

L.G. grabbed Tweet around the collar of his shirt and pushed him across a chair, causing him to stumble back. When Tweet looked up, he was laying on the table with his father inches from his face.

"You listen to me, you stupid, spoiled son-of-a-bitch! You better get your ass in those streets and find my mutha' fuckin money. Do I make myself clear?" He sneered.

"Yeah Pop, I hear you," he replied barely able to breathe.

"Well get yo ass outta here before I put my foot in it!" L.G. snapped as he pulled him from the table and shoved him towards the door.

Tweet stumbled but gained his balance, then walked out of the door at a fast pace. He didn't even glance in Tess's direction. He couldn't believe his father had put his hands on him. He clenched his fist to conceal his anger. When he made it to his car, he climbed inside, slamming the door in the process. "Fuck!" He shouted as he punched at the steering wheel.

* * * *

Flea was sitting on the tailgate of his new Silverado. He had just put a pair of 26's on it and was puffing on a blunt as the hood gave him his props.

"Yo Flea! You eating the streets with this one," one of his young workers said.

Since Tony put Flea on, he had the whole Scottsville on lock. All the so-called Hood Bosses were shopping with him. "Preciate it my nigga," he said to his young worker as he took a pull from the blunt that dangled from the corner of his mouth.

Flea watched as an all-black Mercedes Benz pulled up in front of his truck. He hopped off the tailgate and walked to the front of his ride, making sure the driver didn't get too close. A tall, black older guy got out of the car. He didn't know him, but he was pushing a Benz.

"If you looking for the man, then I'm right here," Flea stated as he stepped up to the guy that stood clearly six inches above him "What's up?" Flea asked the stranger.

"Shit not too much," Oak replied with a calm demeanor. "Just looking for a little something to work with. It's a drought on my side of town and a nigga just tryna eat."

"What side of town you from, homie?"

The Westside, Vincent Village," Oak said, making sure he didn't call out one of their trap houses.

"Yeah, I know a few dudes over there. What you trying to spend."

"Shit! I need a kilo. If you carry weight like that."

"I got whatever you need," Flea said, giving Oak a look that assured him he was talking to the man."

"What's the price?"

"Thirty-four."

"Damn!" Oak said, faking. He didn't give a damn about the price. All he wanted to do was check out the work, but he had to put up a front, so he toyed with him.

"You can't do me no better than that?" he asked.

"She still in the wrapper baby."

Hearing this made Oak seal the deal. "Let's do business then." Knowing he had just made three grand. Flea hopped in his truck. He stopped beside Oak's Benz. "Follow me," he said as he pulled off.

* * * *

Mindy and Meka stood in the mirror as Mindy tried on the dress

Tony had bought her.

"Bitch! This dress is the bomb," Meka said, easing back on Mindy's bed.

"Yeah, it's nice."

So is you gonna give Tony some of that new-pussy?" Meka asked.

"Girl hush. It's not even like that."

"Who you fooling? He just paid almost $400 dollars for a dress, and it's not like that. Well tell me what it is, cause I'll let him ride on this slip and slide for one of those," Meka seriously said, as she rolled her hips in a sexual motion.

"You so nasty!"

"And you better get nasty. Girl, you know that boy been had feelings for you. Like when he stopped Tweet from damn near pulling your arm off."

"I know right!" Mindy exclaimed.

"And now he's paid," Meka said, rubbing her fingers in a money sign motion.

"Is that all you think about?"

"You damn right. While Zack be hitting this pussy, I be tryna think of everything I'mma buy when we hit the mall."

"You wrong for that, ho," Mindy said, laughing.

Mindy thought about the night she heard Zack and Meka fucking. She felt her panties getting wet and was about to take off her dress when her door opened.

"You're beautiful!" Sarah stated as she stared at her daughter. "Where you going?"

"Oh Mama, this is for the Fall fFstival party."

"Well you're gonna turn a lot of heads in that."

"She better, as much as it cost," Meka blurted out.

Sarah walked over to Mindy and picked up the tag. "Mindy! Tell me you didn't pay all this money for this dress?" she asked.

"No, Ms. Sarah. She didn't pay nothing. It was a gift" Meka stated speaking for Mindy.

"Who bought it? That Goines boy? What's his...!" she faked like she couldn't remember. Sarah knew exactly who he was.

"No ma'am!" Mindy answered, finally getting a chance to say something without Meka taking over the conversation.

"Ms. Sarah, Mindy's got a secret admirer."

"I've known him forever," Mindy said.

Sarah knew Tony also. She was also fond of him. He was not a street thug. At least not that she knew of. If it was him that Mindy had a date with, she was fine with it. "Well, I hope you have a good time," she said as she turned to leave.

"Damn bitch! Was you gonna tell everything?" Mindy snapped.

"I heard that," Sarah shouted over her shoulder.

Mindy and Meka looked at each other and burst into laughter.

* * * *

Tweet was riding around still fuming from the shit his father had pulled. Not only did he embarrass him in front of Tess. He took over the meeting, showing the crew he couldn't run the operation.

He fired up a blunt and leaned back in his seat. So far, it had been a rough day. Tweet knew exactly what he needed, some pussy. Seeing Tess's fat pussy had him horny as a mutha' fucka. He was looking around for his phone, when it began to beep.

Right on time, he thought to himself. "Yo, what's up?" he answered.

"Youngblood, this Oak. Meet me at the trap spot on the West side," Oak told him.

"What time?"

"ASAP!" Oak ended the call.

Tweet pulled into the trap spot to find Oak and a few of the workers standing outside. He could see Oak and the Trap Boss were in a deep conversation. As he walked up, they lowered their conversation to a whisper.

"What's up!" Tweet said, feeling like the topic of discussion.

"Come on," Oak said after a moment of silence.

Tweet and Oak walked into the rundown building as the Trap-Boss and his crew followed. The inside of the building was furnished with old furniture. Refusing to sit, once inside, Tweet turned to Oak.

"What's up?" He asked, wondering why he wanted to see him so quick.

Oak studied his face before turning and walking over to the old love seat. He lifted the cushion, pulling out a kilo. Tweet looked at the package that looked to have been open already.

"I opened it for confirmation." Oak said.

"What's wrong with it?"

"Ain't shit wrong with it. Check this out," Oak said as he took the cocaine out the wrapper.

Tweet looked at the coke and saw the L.G.O. stamp on it. "Ok, that's our product," he stated confused.

"I know that, I bought it from a nigga today. This is the work that was stolen from the warehouse Rock operated."

"You sure?" Tweet asked.

"Positive!"

"So what do we do now?"

"I was gonna take it to your father. I know without a doubt by night fall everybody who had something to do with it will be dead, but since you're the boss and this did happen on your watch, I wanted to give you a chance to put a stamp on your name in these streets. Let mutha' fuckas know that L.G. left the operation in the hands of a leader. You feel me," Oak explained.

"I feel you," Tweet replied with confidence.

"The nigga I bought it from, they call him Flea. He had a chain around his neck that said, "The Lick."

Tweet had never heard of that crew. They couldn't be about shit. since the name didn't ring a bell. He didn't give a fuck. The business was gonna be handled. He looked at Oak and held out his fist for a pound.

"Thanks!" He said as he turned and walked out.

Tweet hopped in his car and called Zack. He mashed out in the Camaro, burning up the block.

"Talk to me!" Zack answered.

"The Lick. Have you ever heard of 'em?"

"Nah, it don't ring no bells off the top of my head. Why, what's up?

"What about a nigga called, Flea?"

"Flea... Flea, it sounds familiar, but I can't put a face with the name. What's going on?" Zack asked now concerned.

"That's the nigga that hit my spot."

"Well homie you know I'm loyal to you and your father, so just give me the word."

"That's what's up. Get a team of shooters on stand-by. Let'em know I'm paying top dollar on this one."

"Say no more!" Zack said as he ended the call.

* * * *

"Aaaaw! Right there! Right there! Ooooh," Meka screamed as she was being pounded from the back. She arched her back and squeezed her pussy muscles as her orgasm flowed through her body. Her phone continued to ring, but she already knew it was Zack. He had been calling her for the last two hours.

"Turn over!" Maine ordered.

Meka rolled over on her back, grabbed her legs and pulled them behind her shoulders. Maine climbed on top of her and slid his dick back inside her.

"Oh God! It's too deep," Meka screamed.

Maine started to pound Meka's pussy, letting his balls slap against her ass. She let one of her legs fall, taking away some of his access, but he quickly wrapped his arm around it and pulled it back up.

"Damn, this pussy good," he whispered in her ear.

"Fuck me! fuck me good!" Meka screamed as the pain and pleasure sent her into another orgasm.

She looked at Maine as sweat fell from his forehead and wet up her chest. He had definitely fulfilled the term of beating that pussy up. There was no way she could go another round with him. Zack's ass was out of gas for the next few days. Her pussy was already sore. Not to mention Maine was still inside her hard as a rock. Meka placed her hands on his ass cheeks and pulled him further into her, as she rolled her hips. The warm deep sensation sent Maine and her over the top once again.

"Oh shit! ...I'm cummmmmiinn!" she screamed.

When they both regained strength, Meka rolled over and looked at her phone. She had sixteen miss calls, fifteen were from Zack and one from Mindy.

"I'm out!" Maine said as he walked out of the room.

"I thought you was taking me shopping?"

"Shit, I gotta handle some business. Here you go," he said as he handed her five one hundred-dollar bills.

"Thanks baby!" Meka said as she eyed the money. She picked up her phone and called Mindy.

"So you didn't see my call?" Mindy asked without giving Meka a chance to speak.

"Bitch! You know I was face, down ass up."

"Ain't you always."

"But girrrll! Let me tell you who I was with though."

Meka began to tell Mindy about her sexual escapade with Maine. She told Mindy how Maine had beat her pussy out of commission. As they laughed at Meka's crazy sex scenes, Zack continued to call. Meka finally answered and told him that Mindy was sick, and she had taken her to the doctor. He knew they were close friends and fell for the hook, line and sinker.

CHAPTER SIX

"WHO YOU WITH"

"Step... step a little further." Tony said as he led Tina by the arm. She was blind folded and had no idea where she was.

"Can I take it off now, Tony?" she asked as she continued to take baby steps.

"Almost, a little moe. A... little... moe. Okay stop. On three, take if off. One... two… three."

Tina raised the blindfold and was face to face with a huge Duplex. She looked around at the house, clueless. Finally, she turned to Tony and asked, "Where are we?"

"Home!" he said as he handed her the keys.

"You're kidding me, right?" Tina asked, but then just started screaming and jumping around, all over her brother "Thank you! Thank you! Thank you! Mmmm mmmm mmmm" Tina kissed him on his head.

"Save that shit for Flea," he fused.

Tony's sister had been there for him through thick and thin. When their mother kicked her out because she thought Tina was pregnant by her man, Tony grew to hate his mother then. He hated her even more after the paternity test proved that his sister's child was not his mother's man's baby.

"If Everlyn brings her ass by here. Don't let her in the door," Tony said, speaking of their mother.

"You don't have to worry about that."

Tina and Tony walked through the rooms as she planned how she would decorate the home.

"So which room do you want?" she asked him, giving him the first option, because he did buy the house.

"I won't be staying here."

"Why?" Tina asked with a sad expression on her face.

"Cause, I'll be right next door," he said, pointing to the matching Duplex next door.

"Next door?"

"Yeah, I bought that one too," he said with a smirk on his face.

Tony had purchased both houses through a foreclosure. With the pull of a few strings, along with 150,000 cash, he was able to buy the houses.

"Now, that's what's up," Tina said.

"Well I'm about to go handle some business. I'll catch up with you later," Tony told her as he headed back to his whip.

Tony called Maine as soon as he pulled off. He needed to make sure that their plan was still on for tonight. He had spent a nice chunk of change this week and needed to build his stash back up.

"What's up, gangsta?"

"What's up, my G?" Maine replied.

"What time?"

"First dark. Well just wait it out until they fall asleep."

"That's a bet. I'm out," Tony said as he ended the call.

* * * *

It was almost 2 a.m. in the morning and there were still five cars parked in the driveway.

"All the broke mutha' fuckas gone. All we gotta do now is get in and handle our business," Maine said, looking over at Tony.

Maine and Tony were at John Henry's Gambling House. Maine had been scoping the place out after bringing his uncle to play poker.

"Let's get closer!" Tony said as they crossed the street and climbed on the back of one of the gamblers trucks. From Tony's point of vision, he could see directly through the window. He saw piles of cash on the table and began to put a plan in action. He pulled out the 9 mm Beretta and clicked the safety to on. "Ok," Tony began. "I'm going in the front, you come in the back. Nothing comes out."

"Got'cha!" Maine said as he leaped off the truck and headed towards the back of the house.

Tony waited until Maine was in position. Just as he hopped down, he saw a white Ford Ranger with a Domino's Pizza sign on top of it.

"Perfect!" he whispered to himself, then hopped off the truck and ran over to the delivery guy. "I'm going in, I can take that. Will this cover the cost?" Tony asked, handing the kid a fresh hundred-dollar bill.

"Gee thanks!" The kid said as he passed Tony the pizza boxes through the window.

Tony watched as the kid drove off. He walked to the front door and gave it a light tap. "Pizza delivery!" he called out

"It's about fucking time," a voice boomed from the other side of the door. "I'm fucking starving," the voice continued.

The door swung open and Tony pulled the trigger.

PFF PFF!

The silencer hissed, dropping the doorman immediately. He walked in the room where the gamblers were sitting at a round table. Not one of them looked up from the cards lying on the table.

Anybody order a pizza?" Tony asked behind the mask with a big smile on his face.

"Just sit it..." one of the gamblers said but froze when he looked around and saw the dude in the black ski mask. Ray!" he shouted as the slug threw him out of his seat.

The back door cracked open as Maine came through the dark with only the red beam on his .45 caliber, showing his path as he walked to the table. While Tony was holding boxes of pizza, the gamblers sat with their hands in the air.

"Maine, clear the table!" Tony said as he waited for the first hero.

Maine walked around the table, loading the money into his bag. When he was done, he looked around at the gamblers, walked up to one and pulled him out of his chair. He patted him down, taking all the concealed money and his jewelry.

After checking everybody, Maine turned to Tony and said, "We good!"

"Alright! Head to the car. I'm right behind you."

Maine walked out the front door with the bag. He knew what his partner was about to do. He had told him numerous times that a dead man can't talk or seek revenge. A few minutes later, Tony hopped in the car still holding one of the boxes of pizza.

"You hungry?" he asked Maine as he opened the box and took out a slice. "Shit my favorite, meat lovers," he said, taking a bite.

"Fo' sho, my G," Maine replied as he grabbed a piece then drove off.

* * * *

Flea was sitting on the porch of the trap house. Tina had his truck moving things to their new home. Shit was going good for him now. Tony kept him supplied with all the coke he could sell. As he smoked on a blunt with his crew, he saw a black Camaro pull up to the trap. His crew jumped up strapped and walked to meet the intruders.

"Who y'all looking for?" Dirty Red asked. Dirty Red was a known hothead with a pistol. Flea loved him because he knew all the robbers and want to be Jack Boys. Plus, they knew how he got down.

"We looking for a nigga called, Flea," Zack spoke up first. "What's up? If you want work, produce your money. If we ain't talking money, then I guess we ain't got shit to talk about," Dirty Red snapped.

"I just need to holla at him about some business," Tweet said. Flea sat on the porch and watched as his crew handled business. He didn't know either of the guys or what they could've wanted, if they didn't want work. He had enough killers on standby, so he was not worried about any beef. He pulled on the blunt. *What the fuck they want,* he wondered to himself. "Fuck it!" he said as he hopped off the porch and walked in their direction.

Flea walked through the crowd of young killers, as he made his way to the front. "What's up? You looking for Flea, now you found him," he stated.

Tweet looked at the huge chain that read, 'The Lick.' He looked over at Zack, letting him know that they'd found him. Tweet knew the odds were against them and decided to play on the Boss. "My trap got robbed."

"What the fuck that gotta do with Scottsville... nigga," Dirty Red inquired, cutting him off.

"What I'm saying is the work you selling came from my trap," Tweet said, looking at Flea the whole time.

"I don't know what the fuck you talking about, homie. This little meeting is over," Flea said, turning to walk back to the porch.

"You heard him. This meeting is over!" Dirty Red said, giving them both an evil stare. "And this is the last meeting, anything else is gunplay."

"Have it your way. I was just trying to handle this without bloodshed," Tweet said, as he turned and walked away.

Dirty Red looked back at Flea for the signal. When Flea didn't give him one, he turned and walked back to the porch.

"Why didn't you let me off those niggas?" Dirty Red asked.

They just had the wrong person, Flea thought. Little did he know, he had just made a fatal mistake.

* * * *

Meka and Mindy sat under the hair dryer listening to Bryson Tiller's, *Don't* through the shop sound system.

"That's my jam," Meka said, snapping her fingers. "I can't wait til tomorrow night."

"And who will the lucky man be," Mindy joked.

"Bitch! I know you ain't talking. You better let Tony break that new pussy in of yours."

"It ain't even like that."

"You better make it like that."

"I like him, but I want to take it slow," Mindy said.

"Slow!" Meka snapped. "You keep going slow and watch how fast that nigga end up in another pussy."

"Why you gotta say it so nasty?" Mindy said as she twisted her head to the side.

"Meka, I'm ready for you in chair #1," the stylist said.

"I said it just like I am in bed... naassttyy!" Meka said, rolling her hips and walked off.

"Oooh, I can't stand you!"

"And I love you too," Meka shouted over her shoulder.

* * * *

The Lick

It had been two days since Tweet and Zack talked to Flea. When Tweet had told Oak how Flea and his crew tried to act hard, Oak suggested that they sweep the block with bullets and just put the situation to rest. But Tweet wanted to know who everyone involved was. Even though you can't judge a book by the cover, Tweet just felt that Flea wasn't the type to just take Rock out by himself. He wanted to make everybody involved pay. He pulled up to Top Kut's Barbershop to get a fresh fade, but after he'd circled the block looking for a parking spot, he had to settle for a spot down the block. A little too far to walk to be honest. Tweet was walking up the block when he passed, Styles 4 You Hair Salon. He spotted Meka in the chair with a dark skinned, fat ass chick doing her hair, so he stepped inside and walked up to her.

"What's up, Meka?" he greeted, eyeing the stylist.

"Hey Tweet, where's my man?"

"He's out on the block making some paper so you can stay up in places like this," he said as he looked around and spotted Mindy.

"He better because I need mine."

Tweet walked to the back of the salon. Mindy was still under the dryer. While she sat with her eye's closed, he was tempted to just kiss her, but didn't want to cause a scene. Instead, he sat in the empty seat beside her and placed his hand on her thigh.

Mindy was daydreaming when she felt his hand on her thigh.

"Stop playing bi-," Mindy stated, opening her eyes.

Immediately, she jumped out the chair, hitting her head against the dryer. She thought it was Meka playing a joke on her, but it was Tweet.

"What's up, Mindy?"

"Don't ever put your hands on me again! And what do you want?"

"I just want to take you out when you're done getting dolled up."

"Well that's a dream that's never gonna come true," she snapped.

"Obviously, you must not know who I am? I get what I want," Tweet said, looking her body up and down.

"Mindy, you ready?" The stylist asked.

"Yes," she said, walking past Tweet.

Tweet walked over to Mindy and whispered in her ear, "I like it when you play hard to get."

"Get the fuck out of my face!" she shouted.

Tweet stood back and took one last look before walking off. When he walked by Meka, he winked at her stylist.

"Any time," she said as he walked out.

CHAPTER SEVEN

"TROUBLE IN THE VALLEY"

Maine and Tony sat at the table. They were splitting the money and cocaine from the lick they pulled the night before.

"Yo! This crib tight work, my G," Maine said as he looked around at Tony's new house.

"Shit, you know how we do."

Maine had bought a house a block away from Tony and Tina. They wanted to secure one quarter of the block, but the landlord next to Tony would not sell the property. He had agreed to lease it to Maine, but the crew wasn't looking to rent, only buy.

After handling several business matters, they walked outside. The neighborhood was quiet. Tony looked out at Maine's car. He was driving the new Cadillac ATS-V coupe. The car was black with matching black face 24" Ashanti Rims.

"Don't forget to look into the new lick," Tony said, taking his attention away from the car.

Maine told him about a check cashing store, that cashed checks without I.D. He found out about it, during pillow talk with a bitch. She was into checks and took a lot of her fake one's to the place on a fifty-fifty split.

The store knew what was up and got paid after filing a loss to the insurance company after the check bounced.

"It's ready," Maine replied as they smoked on a blunt.

Tony looked up the street and saw a lady walking in their direction. This was an all-white neighborhood, so to see a black person walking was strange. As the lady got closer, Tony begin to stare. Either his mind was playing tricks on him or this was his mother, Everlyn.

"Yo ain't that your mom, my G?" Maine asked, attempting to pass Tony the blunt.

Tony's face began to frown as Everlyn got closer. She was just how he remembered her. Her face was thin, and you could see her full skull feature. She had lost more hair and was almost bald. Her arms were folded, and she held her head down. She stopped a few feet away from Tony and Maine in silence.

"What the hell you doing over here? I hope you're not looking for no handout cause it ain't happening."

"Why are you talking to me like that? I'm your mother, Tony."

"My mother's dead! Crack killed her a long time ago."

Everlyn knew her kids hated her. But after she heard that Tony bought new houses for Tina and himself, she was surprised. She never knew Tony to be a drug dealer, but was curious as to where he was getting all his money. She had decided to leave it alone. At least they were ok. But Everlyn was in a trap spot on west side when she heard some guys talking about Flea. The talk wasn't good and she wanted to warn him.

"Have you seen, Flea?" she asked.

"Just like I figured... still looking for a high. Get the hell on! And don't ever come back over here. Flea don't sell shit over here."

"I'm not trying to buy nothing."

"Well what the hell you want?"

"I wanted to warn him."

"Warn him?" Tony asked.

"Warn him about what?" Maine cut in.

"I was in one of L.G.'s trap spots. I overheard one of the workers talking about a trap spot in Scottsville. I've been over there before and knew that Flea runs it."

"Okay and?" Tony said, waiting for the warning.

"I heard him say they gonna kill everybody over there.

Something about one of his father's trap houses was robbed and somebody was burned up. Said something about he's in charge now."

Tony and Maine stared at each other. This was the first time one of their licks had resurfaced.

"When was this?" Maine asked. "Last night," Everlyn said.

Tony picked up his phone and dialed Flea's number. He didn't answer. After the third try, he sent a quick text.

Tony: call me...911.

Tony turned to his mother as he placed the phone in his pocket.

"Tony can you buy me something to eat?" she asked as she scratched her arm.

"I'm not giving you a dime!" Tony snapped as he hopped in his car. "Follow me, Maine," he said as he pulled off.

Maine hopped in his car to follow Tony. He looked at Everlyn still standing on the sidewalk with a pitiful look in her eyes. Maine dug in his pocket and pulled out a twenty-dollar bill.

"Everlyn?" he called out.

"Here... it's time to clean yourself up," he said as he pulled off.

* * * *

Dirty Red was sitting on the block listening to 2 Chainz, *Feds Watching*." As it played through his phone, he didn't notice the two limousines when they turned the corner. He finally raised his head as the dark tinted windows slid down.

"What tha' fuck!" he shouted as the gunmen began to shoot.

Pff, pff pff pff!

The silenced machine guns screamed as they rapidly spit fire. Dirty Red only managed to stand up as his body, as well as his phone fell apart.

"Pff pff pff!"

Flea had just walked into the abandoned house when he heard Dirty Red scream. He looked back and saw the cars unloading rounds of fire. He ran out the back door and fled through a neighbor's back yard. He heard his phone ring, but the sounds of gunfire told him he wasn't far enough. After he was at a safe distance, he looked at his phone, saw the 911 text and called Tony.

"Where you at?" Tony asked.

"On the backside of Scottsville. Somebody just shot the block up."

"Go to the small red house at the end of the street. The back door is unlocked. I'll meet you there in five minutes.

When Oak turned the corner, the plan was simple – kill everything walkin... They let off round after round, watching bodies fall. They got out of the limousine, and walked through the abandoned house, but he didn't see Flea. His truck was parked out front, but he wasn't one of the many dead bodies. He walked out and pointed the machine gun at his truck.

Pff...pff...pff...pff!

Sounded the gun as it put over one hundred holes in the truck, causing it to burst into flames. Oak then hopped back in the limousine and pulled off. He sat the gun on the seat and dialed a number. "Done," was the only word that needed to be said.

Oak had given Tweet a chance to handle his business to make a name for himself in the streets, but it had been two weeks since the warehouse robbery. He had talked to L.G. and convinced him to let him handle the business. After the okay, he rounded up the crew and took care of it.

"Good job, Tess," Oak said, looking over at her.

"Thank you," she replied. "Now take me home, so I can get out of this suite."

Tess had on an all-black navy seal suit. She was a sexy accountant to most, but a nightmare to those who made it on L.G.'s blacklist.

* * * *

"What the fuck happened?" Tony asked as he walked into the house. Flea was sitting at the table with a terrified look on his face.

"I don't know, all I know was two limos full of shooters started dumping."

"They killed the whole block," Maine said.

"I gotta go move my truck," Flea said.

"Too late, it's gone, too," Tony replied.

Tony and Maine rode through Scottsville on the way to meet Flea. The police were already beginning to tape the area off. Bodies were spread across the yard as Flea's truck burned.

"It looks like a scene from a horror movie," Tony said.

"Who do you got beef with?" Asked Maine.

"Nobody I know of. These two niggas came by a couple of weeks ago, talking about they had work in our trap. I told 'em they had me fucked up."

"Anything else?" Tony asked. Trying to put the pieces together.

"Oh yeah, and some older nigga bought a kilo. He was driving a black Benz."

Tony looked at Maine, his mother had been right. The trap spot he killed Rock at belonged to Tweet's father. L.G.'s one of the largest drug kingpins in Georgia. Had he known beforehand, he would've turned the lick down, but the damage was done and blood had been spilled. The only way out this battle was through war. L.G.'s organization had money and power. But his crew had heart. Tony thought about the situation, then put a plan in to action.

"Maine, do you know how many trap spots L.G.'s got?"

"Shit probably ten or more."

"Flea, what about you?"

"I used to cop work from a few of them, why what's up?"

"It's simple. They want to go to war. We go to war," Tony said as he walked around the room.

"Let's go," said Tony, walking out the back door. "Flea, ride with Maine. He got tint?"

"What's up, my G?"

"Meet me at Tina's," he commanded, pulling off from the curb.

* * * *

Tony, Maine, Flea and a mob of shooters walked into club 3DL nightclub. They had left the doorman a nice tip, so everybody was carrying heat. Rick Ross's hit, "Colored Money" blasted through the speakers. The last two weeks in the streets had been quiet and the crew was ready to party. It was finally The Fall Festival party and club 3DL was filled to capacity.

Tony was wearing black Polo, loose fitting jeans, a white Polo tee, and a pair of buckskin Polo boots. Maine was behind him, wearing Gucci from head to toe, topped off with a pair of Gucci Aviator sunglasses and the matching watch. The crowd stared as the crew walked through. Every member was wearing a chain that read, *The Lick*. As they entered V.I.P., Tony noticed someone was sitting in their section. He made it to the section and almost lost his breath as he stared in amazement.

"What's up, Mindy?"

"Hello Tony," she spoke softly.

Mindy, Meka, Tina and a few more guests were already partying.

"Let's make a toast!" Tina shouted.

They filled their glasses with Grey Goose and held them in the air.

"To family!" Tina shouted.

"To family!" Everyone said in unison before emptying their glasses.

Meka sat between Mindy and Tina. She could feel Zack's stares across the room. But she never looked in his direction as the crew partied all night. And though on guard, Tony got to dance with Mindy.

* * * *

Tweet and Zack sat across from V.I.P. and watched as Flea partied with Tony and Maine. The pieces of the puzzle were finally coming together. They were all in it together. It didn't matter, because the debt would be paid in blood. The more they watched, the more they were fueled with hate. Not only had they robbed their stash house, but they were partying with two females they wanted, Tweet watched Mindy, who was all up on Tony the whole night. This he took more personal than the drugs.

Zack was watching Meka, but she avoided making eye contact with him. When the girls went to the restroom, she refused to go. This bitch had spent too much of his money to play games. She was not about to leave with another nigga. Zack turned to the table, picked up his drink and finished it off.

"Be right back," he said to Tweet as he walked toward Meka.

"Hold up!" Tweet said, but Zack was already gone. He walked

to the crew who were passing a bottle of Ciroc around, allowing everybody to take a sip.

"Yo Meka!" Zack shouted over the noise of the crew.

Maine looked up when he heard someone call Meka's name. When his eyes met Zacks, he hopped from his seat and stood face to face with Zack who had his hands on his pistol.

"You at the wrong party, homie," Maine said as his shooters surrounded Zack.

"This ain't got nothing to do with you. I just want to holla at my girl."

"This my section. I bought it. So it's got everything to do with me. And furthermore, before you leave, she ain't yo girl."

"Let her tell me that," Zack said, not fearing the crowd that had surrounded him.

"Meka!" Maine shouted, "You got something you want to say to this nigga?"

"No," she said as she walked up and stood behind Maine.

"This ain't over," Zack stared at her.

"It's been over," Meka said, turning to walk off.

Zack jumped towards Meka and was instantly stopped by the feel of metal against his forehead.

"One more step in the wrong direction and it's night night," said Maine as he held his Berreta with a firm grip. "You weren't invited to this party, so walk while you can."

"You got it," Zack said as he backed away from the crowd.

Never taking his eyes off Maine.

* * * *

Mindy had been having the time of her life. The party was live, and she was feeling tipsy. Not only had she been drinking, but she let Meka trick her into pulling on a blunt. She laid back against

Tony. He felt so good, not to mention he smelled awesome. They'd danced earlier and his body felt great against hers. She definitely felt the thumping between her legs. She looked over at Meka, who was eyeing Maine like he was a piece of steak. Meka couldn't throw her ass all over Maine, because Zack was in the building. At least that's what Mindy thought. When the throw back by Luke Skywalker's, *Pop That Pussy* came on, Meka went crazy. She was throwing her ass all over Maine, while Tina shook her small petite frame on Flea. Meka was trying to get Mindy to dance on Tony, but she was afraid the alcohol and weed would throw her off balance. So, she just chilled and watched. So far, the night had been perfect.

* * * *

The lights came on, and the crew headed outside. Tony, Mindy, Flea, Tina, Maine and Meka were surrounded by the shooters. Meka was still grinding her ass on Maine as she walked. His dick was hard, and she could feel it through her skintight dress. As the crowd moved slowly, Mindy walked with her arm around Tony's.

Finally, outside, the crowd was packed in the clubs parking lot.

"Look at all these people," Tina said to Flea.

"3DL is the shit baby. Plus, it's Fall Festival," as they walked toward the cars, Maine saw a crowd standing by his Cadillac.

As they got closer, he noticed Tweet and Zack as well. Pushing Meka to the side, Maine quickly pulled his pistol. He stepped in front of the crew. This was his beef and he could handle it.

"What's up, Homie? You waiting on some problems?" Maine said as he picked up speed.

"We ain't looking for no problems," Tweet said as he stepped up to face Maine.

"I just need to holla at Phony Tony."

"Ain't shit phony about me," Tony said, pressing the remote to his car. "Go to the car," he said to Mindy.

Tweet watched as Mindy walked toward Tony's car. The ride was clean, but he would never give props to Phony Tony. But it was one thing he couldn't deny. There was most definitely a lot of money floating in this crew. Tweet looked at the chain around Tony's neck.

"*The Lick*, huh? I guess you talking about when you robbed my trap spot and killed Rock."

"I don't know what you're talking about," Tony said with a serious face.

"Of course, you do. That's how you and your bullshit crew came up, off us."

"Look, I ain't got time for your games. Plus, I got a little something to handle," Tony said, looking toward his car.

"We'll meet again," Tweet said.

"Any time and any place," Tony said as he walked off.

Both crews left the parking lot. Tweet and Zack had beef with *The Lick*, that went deeper than drugs and money.

"I'm gonna rock those niggas to sleep," Tweet said to Zack as they drove off.

"Not that nigga, Maine you won't. I got something hot for that pussy ass coward."

* * * *

Mindy walked into Tony's house and looked around in amazement, not only was it huge, but everything smelled new. The furniture was still wrapped in plastic. There was a huge flat screen on the wall playing a rerun of, *Martin*. She smiled to herself as she remembered that particular episode.

"Make yourself at home," Tony said as he walked behind the bar in his massive kitchen.

Mindy sat on a love seat and almost lost her breath when she looked up at the ceiling. She could see a full moon that was surrounded by stars. "Wow," was all Mindy could say as Tony sat beside her and handed her a glass of wine.

"To us," Tony said, lifting his glass and gazing into her eyes.

"To us," she repeated with nervousness in her voice.

Mindy slowly sipped her wine. When she lowered her glass, she saw Tony's face advancing towards her. She had kissed a guy before but nothing like tonight. When Tony's lips touched hers, she opened her mouth and allowed him to enter. He gently pulled on her tongue, sending chills through her body. As he continued to kiss her passionately, she placed her hands on his face.

Tony stood and pulled her into his arms. He placed another kiss on her lips, and then he led her to his bedroom. When he opened the door, Mindy felt like she had just entered the *Garden of Eden*. The massive bedroom was beautiful. Like the den, Tony's bedroom gave a full view of the sky. Mindy could literally hear her heartbeat as Tony turned to face her.

"This way," he said, as he walked into the bathroom. Tony filled the jacuzzi with hot bubbling water. He turned to Mindy and began to undress.

"Well, you can't get in with that on."

"I know... but," Mindy started trying to let him know this was new to her.

"No buts," Tony said as he unzipped the back of her dress.

When they were both undressed, they climbed into the water. The air bubbles sent another wave of chills through her body. Tony pulled her across his lap, until she was in the straddle position. He began to kiss her as he rubbed his hands across her soft body. Tony felt the heat from her woman hood as it rubbed against his rock-hard dick. Wanting to be inside her, he placed his hand between their bodies and repositioned himself as the tip of his dick entered her. She jumped from the pain.

"Oooh, Tony," she mumbled.

At that moment, Tony knew what she was trying to tell him.

"Let's do this together. Ok?"

"Alright," she said as she raised her body up for him to enter.

"Oh, God it hurts," Mindy moaned.

After Tony was only a few inches inside, he let Mindy rock back and forth to get comfortable. He continued to take his time, until he had filled her completely. Once inside, they made love over and over as her cries from pain turned into cries of pleasure.

CHAPTER EIGHT

"THE ART OF WAR"

Tweet sat at the head of the table while all the Trap Bosses walked in and joined him. He had overslept because of partying the night before, but his head was clear now.

Tweet had one agenda in mind and that was taking down Tony and his so-called crew, *The Lick*. Everybody was proudly present except Oak. He looked down at his blue face Movado watch. *Where the fuck is he,* Tweet thought to himself.

As he stood to start the meeting, a door opened behind him. Tweet looked back as Oak, Tess and his father stepped out of Tess's office. Surprised by the sight of his father, as well as the fact that they were already having a meeting amongst themselves, Tweet stepped away from the seat at the head of the table.

"Here you go," Tweet said, pointing at the chair.

"Nah, you take it," L.G. said as he continued to stare standing next to Tess. "You called this meeting, so everybody wants to hear what you gotta say."

Tweet stared at his father a second before turning his attention to Oak. He couldn't figure out their agenda but knew without a doubt, with his father always came a motive. He turned his attention back to the table.

"Well, as all of you know, we touched the trap spot in Scottsville," he said as if he had personally orchestrated the hit. "But that mutha' fucker Flea slipped through the cracks. I've also learned that he's not the top dawg of that crew. He's just a fucking soldier. The crew, *The Lick...*" He paused and looked around at his father. "...is ran by Tony and Maine."

L.G. listened as his son delivered his speech. He was quite impressed at the fact that he had finally gotten off his ass and put an ear to the streets. Of course, he already knew this shit. Oak had found this out after he bought the kilo. But he wanted to give his son credit for trying.

The most important part of his speech came now. "What the fuck are you gonna do about it!?" L.G. stood back and waited for his son's orders for retaliation.

"I want them taken out!" Tweet said as he slammed his fist against the table, "Their HO's and all!!" he shouted.

L.G. stepped forward, but Oak grabbed his arm. He knew his son like a book. He wanted to slap this idiot against the head. Once again, he was thinking with his little head and not the big one. *A fucking bitch*, he thought to himself. With the pull of Oak's hand, he fell back.

"Oak, I want that crew *'The Lick'* wiped out," Tweet snapped as he turned to face three cold stares.

"So, what got you so upset?" L.G. asked.

"I saw the crew last night at the club. I tried to talk to Tony, but he was acting like he was the shit."

"Why would you try to conduct business at a club? Nobody's thinking clear at a time like that. Oh, I got it. This nigga Tony had Mindy on his dick all night and you couldn't stand it, uh? Plus, Maine had ho ass Meka throwing her pussy on him in Zack's face."

Tweets facial expression changed. His father had once again peeped his motive. Where the fuck was he? Probably laid up in some young pussy waiting on the report. But fuck it. He was the Boss now and the order had been given out.

He turned to the table, dismissing his father's accusations. He was right but he damn sure wasn't gonna get him to admit it. "The order has been given. Plus, there's a $25,000 bonus on the person that takes Tony out personally," Tweet said as the Trap Bosses walked out.

"Son..." L.G. began, "Do you want to talk about this order you just sent out?"

"What's to talk about?" Tweet said as he followed the crew out the door leaving his father with Oak and Tess. *Yall mutha fucka's talk like you always do. All the secret meetings and shit. I'm about to handle this business*, Tweet thought to himself as he walked past his father.

* * * *

Mindy opened her eyes, but the glare from the sunlight made her momentarily close them again. She opened them slowly, taking in the sunlight as it beamed through the ceiling of Tony's bedroom. She looked next to her, but the bed was empty, so she climbed out of bed and walked into the bathroom. As she sat on the toilet, she looked over at her dress laying on the floor next to the jacuzzi. She began to replay last night. It was amazing. Tony had taken his time and made love to her. It was painful at first, but he made it feel so good. *I can't wait to tell Meka this ain't no "New Pussy" anymore.* Her thoughts were broken when she heard Tony's voice.

"Morning beautiful. How did you sleep?"
"Good morning, Tony. And I slept fine."
"Thank you for a wonderful night."
"No ...thank you," she said in a sexy voice.
Tony leaned down and gave her a soft passionate kiss. "Now

get off this toilet and take a shower. Breakfast is almost ready."

"Breakfast?" she asked with a surprised look.

"Breakfast or bedroom?" he asked with a devilish grin.

"I'll take both," Mindy said as her heart skipped a beat.

Tony and Mindy were into their third round of hot sex when his phone began to ring. Her body had adjusted to him and he felt so good.

"Ooh... don't stop," she moaned.

"It's Maine, I gotta take it."

"He should be taking care of Meka," she said, upset because Maine had interrupted her groove.

"What's up?" Tony answered as he continued to slowly stroke the inside of Mindy's tight pussy.

"Yo', my G. I need to see you ASAP! Meet me at the red house."

* * * *

Everlyn was in line to buy a piece of crack. She thought back as she looked down at the scrapes on her knees. She was laying on her mattress when the well-dressed man walked in her direction. She knew he had money from his gold chain and shiny watch. Everlyn sat up just as he approached her.

"Excuse me, can a sister have a few dollars?"

The businessman looked down at her. She was skinny and he could tell that the crack had taken advantage of her body. But her face still held a nice set of lips.

"Step in the alley," he said after looking around.

Everlyn followed him into the alley. After easing into a secure area, he pulled out his long, limp dick. Knowing what he wanted, she got down on her knees and sucked his dick like her life depended on it. After fifteen minutes with her knees rubbing against the wet cold concrete. She was left alone in the alley with bloody kneecaps and ten dollars. She was in pain, but with a hit of crack, all the pain would be worthwhile.

"Hurry up, Jerome!" A fiend shouted in the line, as Jerome tried to barter with the drug dealer for the most crack he could get with his three dollars.

"Shut the hell up, Slim! I got more than you."

As Everlyn made her way closer to the front, she could hear the drug dealers talking.

"Man, I gotta have them twenty-five stacks."

"Shit, me too, Tweet should've put money on Maine too, then you could've popped that nigga Tony and I could've popped that nigga Maine. Then we both would've been good." Another worker said.

"But fuck it. That nigga Tony's my ticket to becoming a Trap Boss."

Everlyn had just handed her money to the dealer when she heard her son's name. She had to warn him. She had never been there for her kids, but she was not about to let him get gunned down in cold blood. She had no idea what he had gotten himself into, but if it had anything to do with L.G., death was close by. Everlyn took the small piece of crack and walked towards the back of the warehouse to smoke it. When she stepped around the building, she was met by Jerome, who had already smoked his three-dollar supply.

"Let me hit that with you, Everlyn. I'll give you some of this good hard dick," he said, pulling out his dick. He stroked it, trying to get it to rise. "It'll get hard, just watch," he said as he began to stroke faster.

Everlyn thought about her son as she looked down at the crack, and then looked up at Jerome who was stroking his limp dick like he was performing CPR. Everlyn handed Jerome the crack and turned to leave.

"I can't get it up for you Evelyn. But you know Jerome got that long tongue," he said as he licked out his tongue.

Everlyn walked down the street headed to warn her son. She didn't know where he was, but she would walk all over Georgia if necessary. She had to warn him.

Just as Everlyn walked to the corner of Telfair and Jefferson, she saw Maine and Meka walking out of Hop-Inn.

"Maine!" she screamed out at the top of her voice.

* * * *

Sarah was sitting in her living room watching a rerun of Empire. The new security guard had all of Cookie's alarms going off.

"Oooh... Lord Cookie, save some for me!" Sarah said as she picked up the phone. "Hello," she said as if she was the one having sex and had just been interrupted.

"Can I speak to Mindy?"

"She's not here. May I take a message?"

"Yeah sure... Tell her to buy a black dress for that pussy nigga Tony's funeral... But if they happen to be together when I see him, then you have my early condolences, because you're gonna need a black dress yourself," The caller said before the phone went dead.

Sarah sat down at the table. She could barely dial Mindy's number as her heart almost jumped out of her chest.

"Pick up the phone, Mindy!" she shouted as she listened to the operator send her to voice mail. Sarah began to think about her childhood. She would not let anything happen to her daughter. She had promised to protect her. With tears rolling down her cheeks, she grabbed her keys and ran out the door. Sarah didn't know exactly where Tony lived, but she had overheard Mindy and Meka talk about the rich neighborhood over the phone. With thoughts of Meka, she dialed the number she had taken from her daughter's phone for a time just like this.

* * * *

"Oh, what exactly did you hear?" Tony asked his mother.

"I was at the trap house on 42nd when I overheard these guys that work over there talking about how they were gonna collect $25,000 for killing you. I was afraid that something was gonna happen to you, so I gave all my crack to Jerome and left the trap to find you.

Tony looked at Maine and Flea. It didn't take a rocket scientist to know that somebody wanted him dead.

"It's either Tweet or his father," Maine said.

Everlyn looked around the room then stared at her son. "Y'all don't want to cross L.G. That's a dangerous man. I've seen him do some evil things in my days. A while back, L.G. found out one of his Trap Bosses was stealing money. He came to the trap with this fiend name Bazz. Everybody knew Bazz had full blown aids. L.G. held a gun to the poor guy's head while Bazz fucked him. Then went to his house and held his wife at gunpoint while Bazz fuck her too. Word was that when they found out, they were HIV positive, the Trap Boss killed his wife then killed himself."

"Meka, call Tweet and tell him that we want to meet with his father to settle this beef."

"Let me call Zack. Their probably together," she said as she dialed the number and put it on the loudspeaker.

"What Bitch?" Zack answered in a harsh tone.

"Where's Tweet?"

"Why you want to fuck him too?"

"Nah, I'm good. But I got a message for him."

"Talk!" Tweet snapped over Zack's loudspeaker.

"Tony, Maine and Flea want to have a meeting with your father."

"Fuck them! you tell those pussy ass niggas that I run the show! I'm the fucking Boss... and there's nothing to talk about until Tony's mutha fucking dead!" He shouted in a rage.

"I hear you loud and clear," Tony said, ending the call.

Tony stared around the room as he thought about the conversation he just had with Tweet. There was no doubt in his mind that more blood was about to be shed. He eyed Mindy, who was looking as afraid as ever. He didn't want her to hear it, but Maine had called for him to come urgently. As he began to put a plan together in his mind, the sound of Meka's phone went off again. She looked at the number on the screen.

"I don't know this number."

"Just answer it. It's probably Zack playing games," Maine said.

"Hello."

"Meka!" The voice shouted. "Please tell me Mindy's with you."

"She right here," Meka said, recognizing Sarah's voice. She turned to Mindy. "It's your mother."

"Mama?" she answered unsure.

"Mindy! You got to get away from them. They're gonna kill you too. They called looking for you, Mindy. This is serious. Where are you? I'll come get you, baby. Just tell Mama where you're at? Cause they're not gonna kill my baby just like that!" she said, bursting into tears.

"Mrs. Valentine just calm down," Tony said.

"You don't tell me to calm down!! You're the motherfucker they want!! Get away from my daughter!!!"

"Listen," Tony said. I want you to go to the Oconec Apartments Apt 210. In the back by the golf course. It's where Mindy will be staying until this is over. Take everything you need with you because once you're inside the house the doors are self-secured. You will not be able to get out."

"Who the fuck are you?" Sarah mouthed through tears.

"I'm the person that caused this problem. But I'm also the same person that's gonna make it go away."

"Listen to me. You don't know what you're up against. That young kid that's after you is nothing compared to his father. L.G. has power in places you wouldn't believe," Sarah said.

"Thank you. But I've seen a tiny mouse make a giant elephant run," Tony said as he ended the call.

* * * *

It was well after midnight. Tweet and Zack were dressed in all black. It had been three days, and nobody stepped forward to claim the $25,000 reward he had placed on Tony's head. So Tweet, ready for war, had called a crew to meet up at the Northside Trap. "Kill everything moving," was the only order given, they all piled into three vans and pulled off. Tweet and Zack were in the middle van.

"What's the address?" Tweet asked.

"Camp Creek Road," Oak said as he looked down at his phone. "Tony bought two houses next to each other. One was for his sister."

"Okay we'll split up," Tweet ordered. 'I'll take Tony's house. Oak you take a crew and hit the other one."

"Aight."

The men turned into the suburban neighborhood to find it dark and quiet. There was no doubt in anyone's mind that this area belonged to the wealthy. Tweet looked at the neighborhood and was hit with a tinge of jealousy.

He turned to Oak and asked, "Which ones belong to him?"

"The only two with white shutters."

"Right there," Tweet said, pointing at the matching, double car garage homes.

They parked the vans at the end of the block and walked up the street in darkness. After splitting up into groups, they kicked in the doors and entered the homes. Tweet had timed the mission at five minutes in the event the alarm went off. But Tony had slipped up and not activated it.

"Mistake number one," Tweet said as he eased up the stairs.

"I hope this nigga's in the bed with his bitch," he whispered to Zack as he followed closely. Tweet pushed each door open as he walked down the hallway, turning on the lights and checking the closets. When he made it to the master bedroom, he could hear music playing. "Bingo," he whispered.

"We got this pussy," Zack responded.

Tweet cracked the door open. He could see two figures laying in the bed. Tweet pushed the door open and stepped in.

"Goodbye, phony Tony!! He shouted,

Pff pff pff pff - pff pff pff pff - pff pff pff pff!

"Tweet flipped the light on and stared at the bed in disbelief. "Fuck!" he screamed as he stared at the two blow up Betty Boop inflatable dolls. They had been torn apart along with the mattress and walls.

Anger filled Tweets chest as he breathed what could have easily been flames. Tony had played him and he knew it. If this was a trap, then he was in a bad position.

"This might be a trap," he said in panic.

"Let's get outta here!!" Zack said as they ran down the hallway.

After exiting the houses safely, the crew stood out front. Tweet was embarrassed he had been played, but didn't want this crew to see it on his face.

"Burn these mutha' fucka's down!" he ordered.

"You might want to think about this," Oak said so that only Tweet would hear. "This is a residential neighborhood."

"I don't give a fuck!!" he snapped. "Burn it!!!"

* * * *

Tony sat in the trailer of the 18-wheeler watching Maine and Flea pass out guns. They were headed to a Trap house over on the southside. Tweet wouldn't know what hit him when this was over. He had watched them burn down his house. His cell phone home monitor had recorded the entire event. He knew he could never live there again after the war with L.G. and his organization. They turned on Southside and pulled in front of the Trap spot.

The trap boss waved for the driver to back the truck in, thinking it was filled with drugs.

"Let's do it," Tony said as he strapped on his bullet proof vest.

"When the door goes up, the guns go off," Maine told the crew.

The driver backed the trailer to the dock door. Tony could hear the music playing inside the building. When the driver stopped at the door, he saw the Trap Boss walk out.

"You early ain't you?"

"Nah, not according to my schedule."

"Hell, it's ok. I'd rather get it unloaded today."

Tony could hear someone fumbling with the door. When it rolled up, they piled out letting off rounds.

Bac-bac-bac-bac! Boom! Boom!" sounded the guns as the crew dropped bodies.

After about three minutes, the building was quiet, except for the music. Tony looked around and saw that Maine had the Trap Boss at gun point.

"You know I gotta make this worth my time," Maine said, without looking away from his victim.

Tony walked over and slapped the Trap Boss with his pistol. "Where's the mutha' fucking money?"

"Downstairs... just don't kill me. Downstairs in the safe."

Tony walked down the stairs, spotting the safe immediately. "Load everything on the truck, file cabinets and all," he told the crew.

He walked back up the stairs and saw Maine still holding the Trap Boss at gunpoint. Tony walked by and pointed his gun, *Bac-bac!* sounded the gun.

As he continued to walk, he looked back at Maine and the bloody corpse. "Let's go," Tony said as he set the building on fire.

Pulling away from the building, Tony and Maine looked at the money, cocaine, and a file cabinet full of papers.

"You think they want to talk now," Tony said with a smirk.

CHAPTER NINE

"Cat and Mouse…"

"I am not a hostage! I will not be cooped up in this house for the rest of my life!" Sarah complained pissed off.

She had been locked in Tony's Condo for four days and was more than ready to leave. She didn't know what the hell was going on and frankly didn't give a damn. Her only concern was her daughter. She walked in the bedroom where her daughter was laying across the bed.

"Mindy! Call Tony and tell him to free these locks on the doors! This is it. I've had enough, we are leaving!"

"Just calm down, Mama."

"I will not calm down! You either call him or I will be forced to call the police," Sarah said as she stormed out the room.

Mindy watched as her mother left the room. When she was sure she was safe she pulled the phone from underneath the pillow.

"You still there?"

"Yeah I'm here," Tony said.

"So what now?" Mindy asked, knowing it would only be a matter of time before her mother did something stupid."

"I need you to keep her calm. Okay? Now call Meka."

"Okay. Hold on…Meka!!!"

"What's up, girl?"

"C'mere," Mindy said as she motioned for her to lock the door.

"Meka. Can you hear me?" Tony asked.

"Yeah, what's up?"

"Call Zack's phone again. Ask Tweet is he ready to sit down and squash the beef?" Tony said. "Keep it on loudspeaker."

"Alright, hold on," Meka said as she clicked the number."

"What the fuck do you want Bitch? I hope you called to beg for your life." Zack snapped in a nasty tone.

He had been calling and texting her phone all day, but she would not respond.

"Well... not exactly. Tony wants to ask Tweet if he's ready to sit down and squash the beef... y'all... have," she said as she toyed with the word y'all.

"Fuck Tony!" Tweet shouted from a distance. "You tell that mutha fucka he better leave the state if he knows what's good for him. You tell him, I got people everywhere. And when he slips... he won't get up. You hear me, Bitch? You fucking tell him!" Tweet screamed at the top of his lungs before the phone went dead.

"Mindy," Tony called out. "Baby, you gotta talk your mother into chilling for a little while longer. Alright?"

"I'll try, Tony?"

"Okay, Baby?"

"I love you."

Time seemed to have stopped. Tony had been waiting for what felt like a lifetime to hear those words. He knew that he had to get this beef over with as soon as possible because he couldn't wait to hold her in his arms again.

"Tony! Are you still there?" Mindy asked, looking at the reception bars on her phone.

"Yeah, I'm here, baby. And... I love you too, more than anything in this world, Mindy" he said, ending the call.

"Ain't that sweet..." Meka joked not missing a word of the conversation.

"Don't start, Meka! "

"You're my BFF. I'm happy for you," Meka said as she walked to the door and opened it. "Aaaaah!" Meka screamed as Sarah rolled into her feet.

I'm listening!! You act like you don't want me to know what's going on," Sarah said as she brushed off her knees.

"Now did you tell Tony that I am ready to leave this house?"

"Listen to me, Mama. Do you love me?"

"Of course, I do. Why would you ask such a silly question? Why do you think I'm trying to get you out of here?"

"Well Mama, I love Tony. And I'm not leaving his side. So if you love me, you will stay here with me. You're welcome to leave. But I will not leave with you."

"What has he done to you?"

"He loves me, Mama. And I love him too," Mindy said as tears started to fall from her eyes.

Sarah stared at her daughter. It had been many years ago, but she knew that feeling all too well. Even after her mother allowed her to be raped to support her drug habit, Sarah still managed to fall in love with one man. A black man. She was so happy with him. He treated her like a queen. Any and everything Sarah wanted was hers before she could ask for it. This man was her love, her soulmate, her future husband. Until he walked into her home one day and she gave him the news.

"Baby I missed you so much today," she reminisced.

"I miss you so much too," he said giving her a kiss. *"How did the doctor's appointment go?"*

"It was great. I was so happy. I got a surprise for you."

"What is it?"

She'd never forget the look in his eyes when she told him two words. "*I'm pregnant.*"

The love of her life let her body fall out of his arms. He took a step back as he looked down at her stomach, and the words that followed broke her heart beyond repair. "*Well you'll have to get an abortion. My wife can't find out about this.*"

"Mama!" Mindy said, pulling Sarah's arm, allowing her to sit down beside her on the bed.

"He hurt me so bad, baby," she said as tears fell from her eyes.

"I know Mama. But I can't allow your past relationships to dictate my future."

* * * *

L.G. looked down as his dick thrust into Tess. She had one arm around his neck and the other one around his waist. She was sitting on her desk with her legs spread apart as far as possible.

"Fuck me!!" She screamed at the top of her lungs. "Right there... Right there... Don't stop!" she panted between breaths.

The sound of their skin slapping together was driving L.G. crazy. His nuts began to tighten as he thrust deeper and harder.

"Oh shit. Oh shit!" Tess screamed, trying to push some of his length out of her.

"Take it."

"I can't, Baby! It hurts! Aaaah," Tess screamed as L.G. continued to pound her pussy.

She knew he was stressed out; he took all his frustrations out between her legs. He was close to coming, and she was more than ready for him too.

"Let me suck it, daddy." She offered to give her insides a break.

"I just... want... this... good... pussy...," he gasped between short hard thrusts.

"Oh mmyy...GGooo...d!!! Tess screamed as she felt him

explode inside of her.

She wrapped her arms around him as she quietly prayed that he was finished. As he began to stroke her again, his phone went off answering her prayer. As he turned his back to talk in private, Tess took advantage of the opportunity and quickly got dress. She watched in relief as he pulled up his pants.

"What!" L.G. shouted. "You fucking kidding me! Get everybody to the round table now!" He snapped before he threw his phone against the wall.

"What's wrong?" Tess asked in a hesitant voice.

"Another spot got wiped out last night. Everybody's dead.

The fireproof safe was found. But it was empty.

"Where's Maurice? What does he have to say about this?"

"I don't know, but I'm about to find out," L.G. said, looking around for his phone.

He picked it up and called his son.

"What's up, Pop?"

"Don't you what's up Pop me. Do you know another fucking spot got wipe out!" He shouted.

"Yeah, but I burned down his house," Tweet said, trying to impress his father.

"You burned his house! You talking about the two houses that was empty as a mother fucka. Well news flash, we just lost another three million dollars!"

"I'll take care of it."

"No! What your gonna do is get your ass to this round table now!" He said as he slammed down the phone. "Fuck!!!" L.G. shouted, causing Tess to jump back.

* * * *

Tony and the crew of shooters was in the back of the U-Haul truck. Flea was driving as Maine held the map. They turned on Wesley Chapel Road and stopped in front of the warehouse.

Maine could see eight to ten guys leaning over a fat baldhead kid as he threw dice against the wall. The warehouse doors were open as a few guys walked in and out. It was two o'clock and the sun was in full bloom. Tony wanted to make a statement.

Tweet and his father would be ready to talk after today. Flea pulled the huge truck into the parking lot and Maine jumped out.

"Excuse me!" he shouted.

"Mutha fucka, who the fuck you looking for?" A young kid with dirty looking dreads said as he walked up.

Maine pulled out the map and laid it on the trunk of a black Benz.

"I don't want no trouble bra. I'm just a little lost."

"You damn right you lost up in our trap."

"I got a nine to five. Look can you help me find Bartin Hills Apartment's. I got a delivery for a Sunya King. She says it's on Wesley Chapel Road."

"Yeah. yeah, you gotta turn around and go back up one street."

"Can we turn around in here?" Maine asked.

"Sure, no problem. Just get that shit outta here."

"Thanks man," Maine said as he walked back towards the U-Haul.

Flea pulled down to the front of the building and turned the truck into a half U-turn. He looked in the side mirror to level with loading door. Flea let the truck roll back until he bumped the dock wall.

"What the fuck you doing!" Someone shouted.

"A delivery!!!" Tony replied as the door flew up.

PFF PFF PFF - BAC BAC BAC - PFF PFF PFF!

The shooters piled out the truck, killing everything moving. Flea ran inside looking for the owner of the Black Benz. He walked inside flanked by two shooters. He saw the office door and pushed it open.

BAC-BAC!

*S*ounded the pistol.

PFF-PFF-PFF!

Killing the men behind the desk.

"I'm hit!" Flea shouted. "I'm hit!!"

Tony ran in the room and saw Flea on the floor. He pulled him up.

"It's ok. You got on a vest," he shouted. "Is that the guy?" Tony said, pointing at the dead man.

"Yeah. That's him!" Flea shouted.

"Maine, clean out the basement. Get all the documents too. I'm taking Flea to the truck. When you're done, set this bitch on fire."

Five minutes later, the crew was speeding up the road. Flea was laying on the floor shaking. Tony tore his T-shirt and unsnapped the bulletproof vest. He could see the bruise in Flea's rib cage.

"It didn't put a hole in you. It just bruised," Tony said.

"This shit hurt like a mutha fucka!" Flea mumbled in pain.

Tony looked up at the stack of boxes filled with money and cocaine. One thing he knew for sure, this war was making him richer.

After a few minutes, Flea was able to stand up. The vest had stopped the bullet. But the impact of the bullet was still painful.

"I think I gotta get another vest," he said, looking over at Tony.

"Well you definitely got the money to buy one!" Tony said

pointing at the boxes of money.

* * * *

Tweet stepped inside the room to find the meeting had already started. He motioned for Zack to stand by the wall as he walked to the table and took a seat.

"It's about fucking time you got here. Look everybody. It's the man of the hour. The man that was busy burning down two empty houses while a mutha fucka hit us for three million dollars. Let's give him a round of applause." L.G. said as he clapped his hands.

Tweet sat and listened as his father made him feel like shit in front of the crew. How was he supposed to be the Boss, if he was gonna keep pulling shit like this? Tweet looked at Tess who was staring at him through laser eyes. He wanted to ask that snitching bitch what she was looking at. But not right now. That's all it would have taken for his father to blow up further.

"So Maurice, what the fuck is your plan now?" L.G. asked.

As Tweet started to address his father, he saw Zack waving to get his attention. Zack was pointing at his phone with a terrible look   on his face. Tweet's stomach began to knot up, as he felt the pressure from the call. "Not another Trap spot," he said a little too loud.

"Another Trap spot?" Tess repeated.

L.G. walked over to the phone and snatched it out of Zack's hand.

"Who the fuck is this?" he demanded.

"This is Meka. Tony said this is his third and final offer to sit down and settle the beef. If not..."

"Third time.!!!" L.G. snapped.

"Yep... who is this?"

"This is Maurice's father."

"Okay. We've reach out to your son twice to settle this beef. But he continued to say he wants Tony dead."

"Is that right?" L.G. said, looking at Tweet with death in his eyes.

"You tell Tony to name the time and place, and I'll be there."

"No Guns?" Meka asked.

"No Guns," L.G. said as his phone begin to go off. He turned to his son as he looked at the number.

"Hello," L.G. dropped to his knees as the news registered in his brain.

"What is it?" Tess said as she ran to his side.

"The Trap house on Wesley Chapel. It's gone... Everything... Everybody," he mumbled. L.G. looked up at his son.

"If you wasn't my blood, I would kill you right now. Now I want you to get the fuck out."

"Listen Pops -" Tweet began.

"GET... THE... FUCK... OUT!!!!!"

* * * *

"I'm ready to leave this house," Sarah snapped as she threw her cloths into a duffel bag. "I am not a prisoner, and I do have a life."

Tony walked through the house listening to her shout. Even though they were about to settle the beef, he still wanted to keep everybody safe until it was done. But Sarah was determined to leave. Deep down inside, he knew Mindy was ready to return to her normal life too. It had been almost three weeks. But things were starting to look up. With that thought in mind, he decided to let them go.

"Okay. Y'all can leave."

"About time!" Sarah said, cutting him off. She wasted no time grabbing her bags.

"Meka we're gonna need you to stay back as our source of communication. Tina you stay too."

"That's cool," Meka said.

Tina didn't respond. The news didn't bother her because she had her son and Flea there. The bullet he took had scared her to death. Even though he had on a bullet proof vest, just the thought of him getting shot period was too much to bear. Mindy and her mother headed home. Tony had given her a new phone to only call him on. She was to stay low-key and under no circumstances was she to return to work.

They made it home safe and Sarah immediately began to call her friends. She did stick to part of the story regarding them being "out of town." She had a lot of catching up to do and after a hot shower in her own bathroom, she would do just that. Sarah showered and got dressed. When she walked out of the bedroom, Mindy looked at her mother who was dressed as if she had a hot date.

"Where are you going Mama?" she said with a surprised look.

"I will not sit around in this house. Now I'm going out to do some well needed shopping. If you like, you're more than welcome to come."

"We're not supposed to leave, Mama."

"Umph, I'm an adult," Sarah snapped as she walked out the door.

* * * *

Tweet and Zack were walking through the Mall looking for something to freak. His father wasn't talking to him and had regain control of the family's organization. As they passed Macy's, they saw a set of twins walking into the store. Eager to take advantage of the opportunity, they followed them in.

"Excuse me," Tweet called out.

"Yes?" One of the twins said as they both turned around and stared at them.

"I know your time is valuable. But to see two beautiful women was too much to pass by. I was wondering if we could just follow you two around the store, hoping you see something you like." The two smiled, "So we can have the privilege of paying for your items."

"Well it's your money. And I'm very high maintenance," the opposite twin spoke.

"Money's not the problem. I'm Maurice, and this is my best friend, Zack," Tweet said, extending his hand.

"I'm Tamea, and this is my sister, Tamia," she said, extending her hand.

Tweet took her hand noticing the tattoo. He looked at the sister and realized this is how he could now tell them apart.

"Well let's get this started," Zack said, walking towards Tamia.

They walked around the store watching the twins try on different outfits. They each had their own style, and never dressed alike as most twins do. As they walked through the cosmetic section, Zack bumped Tweet, getting his attention.

"What's up?" Tweet said, never taking his eyes of Tamea's ass.

"Look," he whispered.

"That's Mindy's, Mama," Tweet mouthed, not allowing his voice to be heard.

"Tamia, I'm about to step to the bathroom. Here you go," Zack, said handing her $500.00.

Zack walked over and stood against the wall. He could hear Sarah on the phone. Her head was down, and she wasn't paying any attention to her surroundings.

"Child I'm so glad to be out. I just feel so free. Yeah Mindy's fine. She wanted to stay home, so I left her ass right there. I know that's right!" Sarah said as she continued her conversation.

Zack walked away without being noticed. When he found Tweet, they were at the cash register in the urban styles department. "We need to leave now!" He whispered.

They paid for all the items, and then traded numbers with the twins along with promises to call soon. "Double dates on Saturday, right?" Tweet said, as Zack pulled him away.

"We'll be waiting," Tamea smiled, walking away.

"What the hell is wrong with you?" Tweet said with an angry expression on his face.

"Mindy is home alone!"

"Let's go get that Bitch!!!" Tweet said as they hurried out the store.

* * * *

Thing had been quiet for a few days. Tony and the crew were waiting on the meeting with L.G.'s organization. With this beef out the way, things could go back to normal. He thought about Mindy and gave her a call.

"Hey Baby," she answered in a soft voice, "Where you at?"

"Just chilling at the Red house. I was thinking about you and wanted to let you know that you mean the world to me."

"Aww Tony, that's so sweet. You mean the world to me too."

"No Mindy. You don't understand. I've always loved you as long as I can remember. And when this beef shit is over, I don't ever want to have to be away from you again. Ever."

"What are you saying, Tony? You want me to move in with you?"

"I'm saying I...," he sputtered.

"What Tony?"

"I want you to be my wife."

The phone was silent for what seemed like forever. Mindy's lips were moving, but no words would come out. Tears began to fall from her eyes as happiness consumed her.

"Okay. "

"Uh?"

"Okay. Yes," the words escaped. "Yes! Yes! Yes!" she shouted.

"I love you so much, baby."

"I love you too."

Mindy laid back on the recliner as she discussed all her wedding ideas with Tony.

"It's gonna be your day, and your wish is my command," he smiled from ear-to-ear.

* * * *

L.G. walked into Tess's office with a slight smile. She looked up at his gaze because she knew this love making session would not be painful, since he was not stressing or upset with his son. She could feel herself get moist as he closed the door. He took out his phone to make the call that would fix the bullshit his son had caused.

"What's up?" Tony answered.

"Yeah. We can meet at my office at six o'clock."

"No. On neutral ground."

"You have my word. There will be no trouble," L.G. assured. "I don't need your word. I need my life."

"Well, where is this neutral ground?"

"The back side of Scottsville. The last Red house on the block."

"That's the hood."

"You're an old G. You got much respect in the hood. 6 o'clock it is."

"I'll be there," L.G. said as he slid Tess's panties to the side and entered her.

"Oooh," she moaned.

"What's that?" Tony asked.

"Good pussy," L.G. said, ending the call.

"Is it over, daddy?" Tess asked, matching his rhythms with her hips.

"Almost," he replied.

* * * *

Tweet and Zack were outside the window. They could hear someone yelling inside the house. Zack looked through the window. He could see Mindy on the phone. Tweet walked to the back door and twist the door handle.

"It's locked," Zack said.

"Fuck it. It's now or never. If we want that pussy ass nigga to come out, this will do it."

"Let's do it!" Zack said as they kicked in the back door.

Mindy had just hung up with Tony when she heard the loud noise. She made it to the hallway and was met by Tweet and Zack.

"What the hell are ya'll doing in my house!" She asked in fear.

"Just getting some collateral," Tweet said, pointing the gun at her.

"I'm calling the police," Mindy said as she turned to run.

"Get that Bitch!" Tweet shouted as they raced after her.

"Stop! Stop! let go of me!" Mindy shouted as she kicked and fought.

"This bitch crazy!" Zack said, as one of Mindy kicks landed in his nuts.

Mindy kicked and screamed until she felt cold steel. Tweet had hit her in the head. She kicked and fought wildly, until everything went black.

Once out, Tweet and Zack loaded their victim in the back seat of the car. This was sure to even the odds. If his father was thinking he couldn't be a Boss, wait until he saw this. This abduction would definitely get his control of the organization back.

He looked back at Mindy's round ass as she laid in the back-seat unconscious. "Shit, I might get a little something extra."

* * * *

Tess was in a world of bliss. L.G. was the only man she had been with over the last ten years. He made her feel so good. Her body shook as he brought her to her third orgasm. Exhausted from the love making, she was ready to give him the news. Yes, he was married but he loved her. Not to mention, his wife could never make him feel the way she could. Plus, after all, they would be a family too.

"Oooh L.G," she moaned as he came inside of her.

He stroked her until he had released every bit of his juices. When he pulled out, she looked at their mixed fluids as it leaked out of her pussy. Thinking about their future together, she looked up into his eyes.

"L.G.?" she mumbled slightly above a whisper.

"Yes baby?"

"I'm pregnant."

"We'll take care of it later. I have a very important meeting right now. Don't worry. I have a lot of private doctors on call."

"Private doctors?" Tess asked confused.

"We'll talk about it later," he said as he turned and walked out of her office.

CHAPTER 10

"The Red House..."

Sarah pulled into her driveway, acting like she was on stage at the Apollo. Singing R. Kelly's throwback, *I don't see nothing wrong, with a little bump and grind.* She shouted out.

That's the jam, she thought to herself as she grabbed her bags from her shopping spree. Almost forgetting, she grabbed the Citi Trends Bag for Mindy and headed inside.

"Mindy!" she shouted, hoping she would see her hands full and at least open the door for her. With no luck, she freed one of her hands and opened the door. "Mindy!" Sarah shouted, again. "What the hell?" she questioned when she noticed the lampstand turned over. Sarah looked around, as she headed for her daughter's room. "Min..." she froze when she saw that her back door was wide open. She looked down at the broken parts of the door and her heart began to pound in her chest. "Mindy?" she mumbled as she opened her daughter's bedroom door to find it empty. "Mindy!" She cried out in panic. "Miinnddyy!!"

She grabbed her phone and quickly dialed Tony's number. Tears rolled from her eyes as she waited for him to answer.

"Hello?" Tony answered.

"They took her!" Sarah screamed, cry uncontrollably. "They took my baby. Oh my God, Tony. They got my baby."

"Who?" Tony shouted.

"Mindy. They got Mindy!"

Tony's heart stopped. His vision blurred as the realization of her statement set in. They had taken the one thing in this world that he cared about. How could he have fell into their trap. He had been played. He wanted to be strong for Ms. Sarah, but the truth was, his strength was gone. He fell to his knees at the thought of someone harming her. Lost in his thoughts, he was brought back by the screams.

"Aaaahhh! Aaaahh!" Sarah screamed like a woman in childbirth. Tony cleared his head as his mind began to race in overdrive.

"Sarah!" he shouted. "I'm on my way."

Ten minutes later, Tony was standing in Sarah's house listening as she gave him the details of her day. It didn't take a rocket scientist to know that Mindy had been kidnapped. But the question was by whom? He had agreed to meet with L.G. to settle the beef. Tony then looked at his watch. It was four-thirty. The meeting was only an hour and a half away. He didn't know what was happening, but he knew he would get to the bottom of it. Not only for Mindy's life, but his own. If something happened to her, there was no way he could live, nor could anyone responsible for harming her.

"Sarah?" Tony said as he pulled out a .38 revolver from his waist, causing her to jump. "Here, take this."

"What am I gonna do with a gun, Tony? I don't even know how to use it."

"It's simple. You point it at whatever or whoever is trying to harm you or something you love, and you pull the trigger," he said, laying the gun on the table.

"I'm scared, Tony."

"It's okay to be scared but be safe. Now take the gun," he said as he turned and walked out of the door. He pulled out his phone and call Maine.

"What's up, my G?"

"They got Mindy," he said in a defeated voice.

"Who? What the fuck happened?"

They took her from her house. I'm not sure who's responsible.

Let's go to the meeting. If L.G. don't show, then we'll have our answer.

"Then what?" Maine asked, knowing his friend all too well.

"Then we'll raise the body count of his operation even more."

"I got everything set up. Once they walk into the house, it's up to us if they make it out."

"That's what's up."

* * * *

Mindy opened her eyes and looked around the room. The smell of weed smoke was strong and she could hear voices in the next room. She was tied to a chair with her mouth tape closed. "Mmm-mmm-mmm," she mumbled.

She rocked the chair back and forth, causing it to fall over.

"Mmm!!" she moaned from the pain of hitting her head against the floor.

The door opened and a shadow crossed her body.

"Well, well, sleeping beauty has awakened. Was you going somewhere?" the voice asked as it pulled her chair up right.

Mindy looked up and her worst fear became true all over again. Tweet was standing in her face. He was wearing nothing more than a pair of boxers. He pulled the tape from her mouth, and engaged her in idol chatter.

"It's hard to talk with all that, huh?" he said with a smirk.

"What do you want, Tweet?"

"What I always wanted, Mindy… you."

"Well that will never happen," she snapped.

"Don't be so sure of yourself. Ya see right now, I'm calling the shots."

"When Tony finds you, you're dead, Tweet."

Wamm! Tweet slapped Mindy, knocking blood from her mouth.

"Don't you ever threaten me with that pussy ass nigga again!"

"He's more man than you'll ever be, Tweet. What you gonna do, rape me? Huh Tweet? You gonna rape me? Well come on damn it! Take it like the pervert you are! But you know what? I'm still not gonna want you. And I'm still gonna love Tony."

Wammm!

"Shut the fuck up!" Tweet yelled as he slapped Mindy again.

Dazed from the blow, Mindy raised her head up. She knew that Tweet was easy to manipulate. His plans were to rape her, so the longer she kept him fighting her the better chance she had at not being rape by him. With that thought she continued, "What's wrong, Tweet? The truth hurts?" she mumbled through a busted lip.

"Tweet?" Zack yelled out as he walked to the door.

"One minute. I'm on my way out."

* * * *

L.G. pulled in front of the old abandoned house and looked around. This shit was definitely in the hood. As he continued to scan the area, he looked over at Oak.

"What do you think?" Oak asked.

"I think it's time," L.G. said as he pointed to the women as she walked out the front door.

"This a crack house?" Oak asked, looking at the skinny women walking in their direction.

Everlyn walked toward the car. She looked down at the two, recognizing L.G. as the driver.

"Where's Tony?" Oak said as he rolled down the window.

"He's on the way. He said to tell you to come in."

"We'll wait out here," Oak said as he began to look the neighborhood over again.

"Okay, suit yourself. But it's a lot safer inside. Sitting inside of a Cadillac Escalade in the middle of the hood can draw unwanted company," Everyln said as she pointed at the young drug dealers down the street.

L.G. looked down at his watch. It was 5:45. Fear was not a factor for the old G. But he didn't make it this far in the game without making sound decisions. He knew the rule was no guns, but his instincts told him this was far from neutral grounds.

"Pack up." He told Oak as he stuffed his berretta inside his shoulder holster and opened the door of the SUV.

L.G. and Oak followed Everlyn toward the rundown house.

"How many people are there on the inside?" L.G. asked, stopping at the entrance.

"Nobody. It's just me," Everyln said, never looking back.

They stepped into the rundown house and were surprised by what they saw on the inside. The walls were decorated with portraits of legendary African Americans hanging about. L.G. took in the scenery and was impressed with the selection. He walked up to a portrait of Barack Obama and knew it was costly, being that it was a replica of an original one hanging in the Oval Office.

"Pretty incredible guy, uh?" Tony said as he watched L.G. from across the room.

L.G. and Oak turned simultaneously, pulling their weapons on Tony.

"Aaah!" Screamed Everyln as she jumped in front of her son.

"Well I see you broke the first rule," Tony said as he stepped around his mother.

"I don't take orders. I give 'em," L.G. said with his gun still aimed at Tony.

"Well I guess we've got a problem, cause I don't take orders either.

"You must don't know who I am?" L.G. snapped.

"I know exactly who you are," Tony said, pulling out a stack of paper.

"You're Larry Goines. You received 200 kilos at the warehouse on Welsely Chapel Road in the months of January, February..."

"Let me see that shit!" L.G. said, snatching the papers from Tony.

"How the fuck did you get this shit!" He said as he glanced at Oak. "I should just kill him right now and get it over with."

"You can kill me right now, but it's far from over. Take a look," Tony said, pointing at the flat screen as he turned it on.

"Maine can you hear me?"

"Loud and clear, My G," Maine said, giving Tony a thumbs up from the screen.

"Show'em what we got."

Maine pulled a stack of boxes in front of the monitor, revealing more documents of the Larry Goines operation.

"Oh, my fucking God!" L.G. shouted as he watched the screen.

He knew without a doubt that his life was in the hands of these young thugs. If they were looking for money, then he was willing to pay them.

"How much?" L.G. asked as he continue to stare at the screen.

"How fuckin much!?"

"See that's where you're wrong, L.G. I don't need your money. You got something much more valuable to me than money.

I want this beef you got with my crew and the hit your son put on my head dead."

"I never had a problem with you. You came after me, remember. You hit my trap spot and killed Rock," L.G. reminded him.

"We didn't know it was your spot."

"I tell you what. You can keep the money and the cocaine. Just give me the documents," L.G. pleaded.

"And we will forget all this," Oak added.

"You have something much more important than the money L.G. You have my girl. And unless you want Uncle Sam's employees at your front door, you got one hour to deliver her here," Tony growled.

"What the hell are you talking about?"

"You know what I'm talking about! Mindy! You took her motherfucker!" Tony said, walking up to L.G.

"My word is always good in the streets. I know nothing about your girl."

L.G. stood face to face with Tony. He had no clue what Tony was talking about. He looked at Oak for confirmation.

"We know nothing about the girl," Oak confirmed.

Bzzz-Bzzz-Bzzz, vibrated L.G.'s phone. *Bzzz-Bzzz-Bzzz...*

L.G. looked down at the phone and saw his son's picture on the live screen.

"I don't know anything about your girl. This is my son. Listen, I'll prove it to you," he said as he took the call.

"Son, where are you? You supposed to be at the meeting. We're waiting on you."

"Fuck the meeting!" Tweet shouted. "I got something much more important than that bullshit ass meeting. I got this," Tweet said as he turned his phone to Mindy.

She was sitting in a chair with her arms and legs wrapped in duct tape.

"Say hi to the camera," Tweet said as he pulled the tape from Mindy's mouth. Tony couldn't believe his eyes. His blood raced through his veins as his heart jumped out of his chest.

"Mindy!" He shouted.

"What the fuck are you doing?" L.G. shouted. You fucking idiot!"

"Fuck a meeting!" Tweet shouted. "If those muthafucka's wanna go to war, we can start right now!"

"Let her fucking go!" L.G. screamed at his phone.

"Nah Pops. I can't do that. See that's where we're different. You always want to work it out so that everybody can be happy. But sometimes Pops... It's not always gonna be a happy ending."

* * * *

Sarah had been watching the hotel for four hours. Other than a new black Camaro parked out front, the hotel was fairly empty. Sarah had found the location by tracking Mindy's phone. They were on the same contract, so with a call to the tracking center, she was able to pin-point Mindy's location. She looked down at the gun Tony had given her. Her heart began to beat faster, thinking about her past. She had been raped, beaten, and abused. It would not happen to her daughter. She opened the door and froze. Sarah could see two men talking. They were too far away to hear the conversation, but the hand gestures told her it had to be something serious.

"Mindy. Mama's gonna protect you," she said to herself.

Sarah watched as one of the guys climbed into the Camaro and sped off. The second guy nervously looked around and walked back into the room. She took out her phone and texted Tony.

Sarah: The Marriot on Washington Road Room 219.

Sarah pushed the pistol down inside her oversized purse. She tied a scarf around her head and put on a pair of dark sunglasses. She looked in the mirror one last time and climbed out of the car. She walked across the parking lot with her hand on the pistol. Sarah saw the maid as she pushed a load of bed linen. The maid opened a closet door and pushed the cart inside.

Sarah walked to the closet door and stepped inside. She immediately saw the key card on the cart. Room service use only. She took the cart along with the key card and headed for room 219.

Tweet stood in front of Mindy with nothing on but his boxers. He pulled her out the chair and pushed her on the bed.

"So I guess your gonna rape me uh?"

"Nah Bitch. I'm just gonna show you what a good fuck feels like, so shut the fuck up!" Tweet shouted, slapping Mindy across the face.

"Stop! Stop! Stoopp!!" Mindy screamed as she used all her strength to keep from opening her legs.

"Bitch... you can fight... all... you want to!"

"Help... Help! Oh... My... God... Help." Mindy screamed as she felt herself being overpowered. She could feel his manhood between her legs. Struggling, Mindy continued to fight to keep her legs together.

Wap!

Tweet slapped her again, knocking her in a daze.

Her body stopped and her legs fell apart. "Bout time bitch."

"Nah it's past time mutha fucka! Get off her!"

* * * *

Meka was standing in the kitchen when she heard the knock at the door.

"Who is it?" she called out.

"Maine, is that you?" She looked through the peep hold and her heart almost stopped. *They're here,* she thought to herself. "They've come to kill me like they did Mindy," she said to herself. Meka stepped away from the door as the knocking continued. Not wanting to panic, she grabbed her phone and called Maine. "Who is it?" she called out as she waited for Maine to pick up.

"Open the door!" Zack called out. "I just want to talk to you!"

"What's up?" Maine answered.

"Maine," Meka whispered. "They're over here. Zack is at my door."

"I'm on my way. Don't open it!"

"What do you want, Zack? Why are you here?"

"I just want to talk to you, baby. I miss you. It'll be like old times, you know," he said with his hands on his pistol.

"It's over Zack. We have nothing to talk about."

Bac-Bac-Bac!

"Aaaah!" screamed Meka as she jumped back, falling over the sofa.

"Bitch it ain't over til I say it's over!"

"Go away Zack!"

Bac-Bac-Bac Bac... Bac-Bac!

Zack continued to shoot at the door until it was barely standing. He kicked the shattered wood, causing it to break like a toothpick. Stepping through the debris, he looked around the room. Meka was lying on the floor with her hands over her ears.

"Get the fuck up, Bitch!"

"Aaaah!! Your hurting me!"

"Yeah Bitch, at one time, I used to love it when you told me that. But you had to switch sides. What the fuck you thought? I was something to play with? You thought you could just spend a nigga's money and say fuck 'em? Nah, Bitch. Two can play that game."

"I'll pay you back, Zack. All of it. I promise, just don't hurt me."

"You want to pay me back?"

"Yeah. Anything. Just please don't hurt me."

"Aight, bitch strip!" Zack said, pointing the pistol at Meka's head. "Strip, Bitch!"

Meka stared at the man she once loved. He had seen her naked so many times. But this time she felt dirty, as she slowly began to unbutton her pants.

"I ain't got all day. Hurry the fuck up!"

"Okay... just don't hurt me," she cried as the tears fell from her face.

When Meka was totally naked, she stood in front of Zack. She was shaking in fear, as he stared at the women he once loved with pure hatred.

"Lay on the fuckin' floor."

"Okay Zack... I'm going," she whimpered.

Zack stood over Meka and peered down at her naked body. He took out his dick and aim it at her mouth. "Open up."

"No Zack... please don't make me do it."

"It's either in your mouth or in your ass, bitch. And you better choose fast, or I'm taking both." Zack snapped as Meka slowly opened her mouth. Zack sat on Meka's chest while his dick touched her lips. He looked down at her and realized just how much he hated her.

"Take this, bitch..." he said as he began to piss in her face.

"Aaaah!" Meka screamed as the hot piss burned her eyes.

Zack slid down her body, as she tried to wipe her eyes. He shoved his dick inside her in one stroke, forcing her to scream out in pure pain, "Aaaah!!!"

Zack continued to fuck her with no remorse. He pushed his dick as far into her pussy as he could. Meka screamed as she felt her insides being ripped apart. When Zack was done, he stood over her as semen and blood dropped from his dick. "Now, he can have you, ho," he said as he pulled up his pants.

CHAPTER ELEVEN

"The Demon of Death..."

Tony was standing face to face with L.G. He watched Oak out of the corner of his eye as he contemplated his next move. He could go for his pistol and surely kill one of them, but the odds were not in his favor.

"Trust me. I had nothing to do with this," L.G. said.

"At this point, it don't matter. If something has happened to Mindy, I'll turn every stone on the face of the earth until I find you and kill you."

"I don't take threats too kindly."

"And I don't make 'em. It's a promise L.G. I got enough shooters around this house right now to go to war against Iraq."

"Just give me a chance to fix this."

"The clock is ticking," Tony said as he stepped away from L.G. "Show yourself out."

"What about your shooters outside?" Oak nervously asked.

"Hope it's your lucky day."

Tony was on his way to the hotel at full speed. He was so caught up with L.G. that he missed Sarah's text. His mind was moving faster than his car. If Tweet hurt Mindy, he would kill him. It didn't matter who his father was. The traffic was so backed up, Tony drove in the turning lane. When he made it to his turn, he made an illegal left that could've cost him his life. It didn't matter, he had to save his girl. He saw the Hotel's sign up ahead. Tony could feel the hair on his neck stand up. His heart dropped to his stomach and his breaths became short. As he turned into the parking lot, he said a short prayer. "God, I haven't talked to you lately. I used to pray to you all the time when I was young. Remember? I used to ask you to let my Mama come home safe, when she was out smoking crack. But I'm back again. I need a couple of your angels to watch over Mindy. Don't let harm come her way. Take care of her until I can do it myself. Amen." Tony said as she stepped out the car.

* * * *

Sarah push the door open and all the memories of her childhood flooded her mind. She saw men having sex with her mother, and she relived men raping her. As she stared at Tweet on top of her daughter. *I'm gonna protect you, baby*, she thought.

"Aaaah!" Mindy screamed out.

"Get your ass off of her!" Sarah shouted as she raised the gun.

Tweet jumped off Mindy as soon as he heard the voice behind him.

"If you know what's good for you, then you will put that gun up, get the fuck outta my room, and let me and my girl handle our business."

"Your girl? Your fucking girl!? You meant to say your sister, you rapist bastard!"

Sarah closed her eyes as Tony's words replayed in her head. *It's simple. You point it at whatever it is that's trying to harm you or something you love...* and you pull the trigger. "

Bac-Bac-Bac!

"Aaaah!!" Screamed Mindy as Tweets body fell to the floor. The sound of his screams along with Mindy shaking her brought Sarah out of her comatose state.

Tony stepped inside the room and wrapped Mindy in his arms.

"It's okay. It's okay. I'm here now," he whispered in her ear.

"He was going to rape me," she said as she continued to cry.

Tony looked up at the two holes in the wall. He knew he heard three shots. To his right he saw Tweet clutching his right shoulder. The blood running down his chest made a pool in his navel area.

"Help! I need a doctor!" He grunted in pain.

"Give me the gun," Tony said as he turned to Sarah while she continued to stare at Tweet. "Sarah," he said, causing her body to jump. "Please... give me the gun."

"Mama please. Just put the gun down," Mindy begged in tears.

"He was gonna rape you. Like they did me. But I promised you that I would protect you, baby. I can't let him live. See a rapist won't stop. They are like cancer. They take, and take, and take, until there's nothing left. Then when they're done with you, they leave you with the memory and it continues to rape you over and over."

Bac!

"Don't!" Tony shouted as he pushed Sarah's body. He wrestled with her wrist trying to take control of the gun. "I can't let you do this Sarah!" he said as he continued.

Bac-Bac! sounded the gun as Sarah pulled on the trigger.

Tony looked into her eyes and knew that she would kill Tweet if he didn't stop her. Even though he could kill him with no remorse, he didn't want that demon to haunt Sarah. The demon of death was a spirit you met after you took a life. He followed you every hour of every day and reminded you that you're a killer. He couldn't let her do it.

Wamm!

Sounded his fist as he knocked her out cold.

The pistol fell freely from her hands. Tony picked up the pistol and turned his attention to Tweet. He could see the fear in his eyes as he picked Sarah up.

"Let's go." He said to Mindy as he walked out. "Hey! I need a doctor!" Tweet shouted.

"People in hell need ice water," Tony said over his shoulder without looking back.

* * * *

Maine jumped out of the car and ran through what was left of Meka's front door. He pulled out his pistol as he walked down the hall.

"Meka!" he shouted. As he opened each door, he passed.

Maine pushed the bathroom door open and his heart almost stopped. Meka was leaning against the tub with her knees folded against her chest. Maine looked at the blood on the floor and rushed to her side.

"Are you shot?" he said, as he looked over her body for a bullet wound. "Meka, talk to me. Are you okay? Are you shot?" he asked as tears filled his eyes.

She nodded her head from side to side as she tried to open her mouth. The words were too heavy. *Who would want to be with me after my body was no good,* she thought to herself. She looked up at Maine as her mind flashed back to the things Zack had done to her.

"Get away from me!" she screamed as she swung her fist wildly. "Get away from me. Get off me. You're hurting me... Zack stop it!"

Maine hugged her tightly, taking every blow as if it was his fault. He knew where the blood had come from. She had been raped. Zack had raped the women he loved, and he would pay with his life. He picked Meka up as she continued to fight. He walked her into her bedroom and laid her on the bed, wrapping the sheets around her naked body. He picked her up again and headed for the door with her in his arms.

It had been two hours and the doctor still hadn't returned. Maine paced back and forth. Tony had found Mindy, so things were somewhat better. Now if the doctor would just let him know something. While he waited, he thought about his mother and grandmother. They were devoted Christians and Maine was no stranger to Jesus Christ. With nothing left, he got down on his knees.

"Jesus... I know you're up there. I've done some things that I'm not proud of. But you said that you're a God of forgiveness. I ask for forgiveness for the sins I have committed. And if my sins are too much to just throw into the sea of forgetfulness, then take my life and let Meka live. My heart is set to kill Zack, but I know you already know that.

"Maine... Maine are you asleep?" a voice said.

Maine looked up at Flea, Tina and Tony.

"What are y'all doing here?" he asked as he jumped to his feet. "I was just talking to the man upstairs," Maine said, pointing at the ceiling.

"Any word yet?" Flea asked.

"Excuse me," a small white man with a bald head interrupted.

"Are you Tameka Williams' family?"

"Yes," Maine said.

"Mrs. Williams is going to be fine," the doctor said as he watched the family breathe a sigh of relief. "But, being rape is not something you forget overnight. Some people are strong and can put it behind them, but for others... it can haunt them for a lifetime. She will need lots of moral support, during this time."

Tony thought about Sarah and how she had tried to kill Tweet. He understood fully what the doctor was talking about.

"Can we see her now?" Maine asked.

"Yes, I'll make an exception this time," the doctor said, looking down at his watch.

* * * *

Tess sat behind her desk as L.G. continued to explain to her how his son had put, not only his life, but his freedom in jeopardy. His words went in one ear and out the other. The only thing that was on her mind was the baby she was now carrying in her stomach. If he thought for one second that she was gonna kill her child, he had better think again. Hell would freeze over first and he would definitely have to take her life as well.

"Tess... Tess... you hear me talking to you? I said I just got word that Maurice was shot! Let's go!" L.G. said as he turned to leave.

On the way to the hospital, Tess stared out the window. As L.G. continued to talk, she needed to know just where they stood with her child. She knew this was not the best time. But her motherly instincts were running wild.

"So what about the baby?"

"What do you mean? What about the baby? We talked about that. I got the best doctor. They will take care of it. Matter of fact, we can take care of it when we get to the hospital. You know, kill two birds with one stone."

"I'm not killing my baby," Tess said in a whisper through clenched teeth.

"You do what the fuck I tell you to do!" L.G. snapped as he attempted to back hand her.

Catching his hand in motion, Tess turned her full body toward L.G. "If you ever raise your hand at me again, I will kill you."

"You can't have this baby!" he said as he snatched his arm out of her grasps.

L.G. knew that Tess was dangerous. She could kill a person in less than a minute. He would have to come up with a plan to get rid of this baby. A plan that's mistake free. As they walked into the hospital, he was immediately met by his private doctor.

"This way Mr. Goines," the doctor said as he led him towards the private elevator.

"How is he?" L.G. asked as he looked over at Tess's stomach. "He's fine. The bullet went straight through his shoulder."

L.G. walked into the room and saw his son talking on his cell phone.

"Get off the fucking phone!" he said, grabbing the phone and slinging it across the room. "Everybody out!"

L.G. glared at Tweet as the room cleared out. He knew about everything his son had tried to do to Mindy. To keep the beef from starting again, he had met with Tony a second time. Plus, he still had the documents to his organization.

"What the fuck was you thinking!

"I was gonna keep the bitch until they turned over the documents."

"You're fucking lying!" L.G. said, striking his son across the face. "You tried to rape her!"

"So fucking what!? She ain't shit!" Tweet shouted.

"You stupid mutha fucka!" L.G. said, wrapping his hands around Tweet's neck. "I should just kill you my damn self and get it over with."

"Mr. Goines!" The doctor called out as he burst through the door. "You're gonna kill him!" he continued as he watched his patients face turn blue.

"That's my intention."

After his hands were forced from Tweet's neck, he backed out of the room to a waiting Tess.

"Hey Doc," he called out.

"Yes, Mr. Goines?" the doctor answered, stepping outside of the room for his patient's safety.

"I have some private work for you," he said as he looked towards Tess's stomach.

"Just give me a call, and I'll schedule you an appointment."

"That won't be necessary," Tess snapped as she turned and walked away.

"Where are you going?" L.G. called out behind her.

"Go fuck yourself, L.G."

"You're fired!"

Tess stop and turned to face L.G. "No… I quit!" she said as she pulled out her phone to call a cab.

"Women...can't live with 'em, can't live without 'em," L.G. said as he turned his attention back to the doctor.

* * * *

Mindy was laying across her mother's lap with a million thoughts going through her mind. She couldn't forget her mother's words inside of the hotel room. Was she just talking? Did she really mean her brother? All her life Mindy had always thought she was an only child.

"Mama?" she mumbled.

"Yes, baby."

"Is he really?" she said, lifting her head to look into her mother's eyes.

"Really what?"

"You know... Is he really my brother?"

Tears fell from Sarah's eyes. She knew that one day this dark secret would come to light. She had done everything she could to keep it buried. But the time had come. The rejection, the pain, the fear of him finding out that it's in the open. Everything. It was about to come out. She would not lie to her daughter any longer. She deserved to know who her family is and more importantly, she deserved the peace. Sarah looked into her daughter's eyes as she took a journey down this dark path for the final time.

"I was so young. And he was my first love. I loved him so much and he loved me. Or at least that's what I thought." She began, as the tears continued to fall. "He walked into the apartment he'd gotten for us, and I told him I had a surprise for him. I told him I was pregnant, and he just dropped me out of his arms as if he didn't know me. The look in his eyes was totally different."

Sarah couldn't continue. She hugged her daughter as they both shed tears. The pain was as fresh as yesterday. She had to continue. She owed it to Mindy. But most of all, she owed it to herself. She took a deep breath and exhaled.

"Then he told me to get an abortion because his wife couldn't find out about his affair with me."

"And what did you do, Mama?"

"The next day I packed all my stuff. I knew that he had money in a safe in the closet, so I took every dime out of it and got on the next bus out of town."

"Where did you go?" Mindy asked.

"Atlanta. I got a job at a Home Health Care agency until you were born. After you were old enough to go to the nursery, I returned to work. I stayed there until you were five. The company folded, so after a call to some old friends, I came back home."

"So he don't know I'm his daughter?"

"He knew... but by this time, he had a lot of money and began to pay me to keep quiet, especially after I threatened to go to child services."

"So what did you do?"

"I was barely making enough money to pay the bills, baby. So I took the money. I'm so sorry," Sarah said as she hugged her daughter. She felt so much better now that the weight of her past had finally been lifted. *At least some of it*, she thought to herself.

* * * *

Tess paced back and forth in her bedroom as she thought about L.G. trying to kill her unborn child. *All these years he told me he loved me, and I've been faithful as hell to his black ass. Gave him my all, and this is what I get in return.* "Aaaahh!!" she screamed as she looked in the mirror.

Her hair was wild, and her makeup was gone. Being pretty was the last thing on her mind. The hairs on her arm and neck stood up as her blood began to boil. Tess was no stranger to this feeling. She had felt it many times in her life. And the results were always the same. Death. Somebody was about to die. She thought back to her childhood.

Her stepfather used to make her kiss the "Little Man", as he called it. When she graduated, she joined the Navy. She took all her frustrations out in the training fields and graduated at the top of her class. She joined a secret society of Navy Seal Snipers where she learned the art of war, and most of all – how to kill. Tess was brought back to reality when she heard a noise. She quickly turned off all the lights, taking the advantage of sight away from her enemy.

L.G. sat up the street and waited while two armed men set out to get Tess. She couldn't have this baby. He knew that she was angry, but she would thank him later. He knew she was dangerous, too, so he chose his top security soldiers to go get her.

Tess stood still in the middle of the dark room. She watched as her intruders made their way to her bedroom. Just as she expected, they split up. A fatal mistake. She walked down the hall with steps like those of a cheetah. Tess stood behind one of the men as he searched for the light.

"It's right here," she said as she twisted his neck 180 degrees, killing him instantly.

"Mike... Mike can you hear me?" the second intruder said.

"Uqaah!" Tess grunted as she side kicked him, causing his gun to fall to the floor.

She karate chopped his neck on both sides, cutting off his air.

"Don't kill me!" he mumbled.

"Now that won't be lady like, would it?" she said as she ripped his Adam's apple out of his throat.

Tess walked into the darkness. She could hear the sound of L.G.'s engine. She walked to the front of the car and in one step leaped on the hood.

Boc-Boc-Boc-Boc!

She fired through the windshield, killing the driver. After which she leaned down through the broken glass.

"You looking for me?"

"We need to talk," L.G. said, trying to hide his fear.

"Talk... and if I don't like what you say, then you'll join the two that you sent for me and this fat piece of shit," she said, letting off another shot.

"It's about the baby."

"Keep going," Tess said as she pointed the gun at L.G.

L.G. looked at Tess as she held a stare without the first sign of fear. He knew that she would kill him if he wasn't careful.

"I thought you loved me. "

"I do. But I love this child more. Now if you want to hear the birds sing in the morning, I suggest you get that trash out my house and never return. Do you understand?"

"I got you," L.G. said, nodding his head.

Tess jumped from the hood, turned and walked away.

CHAPTER TWELVE

"Rules..."

"I'mma kill 'em, my G... I swear to God I'mma make that nigga pay for this shit," Maine said, as he looked down at Meka.

"Don't worry about those niggas, Maine," Tony said. "I got something for all of 'em. Just trust me."

"Yeah, I can't wait to let that fire go on them mutha fucker's," Flea joined in.

"Baby, I promise. I won't let that nigga get away with this. That's on my life," Maine said, squeezing Meka's hand.

Meka looked around the room at the faces. She recognized everyone there, but her mind was still in shock. She was afraid to close her eyes, fearing that her attacker might return. The doctor injected a strong dose of pain medicine to lessen the pain from the stitches that held her insides together.

"We need to hit the streets," Tony said, placing his hands-on Maines shoulder. "Let's go handle this business," he encouraged.

"It's about time," Flea said as he adjusted the .45 in his pants.

"Please... pleeaaase... pleeaase... don't leave me!" Meka screamed out in tears.

"It's ok... It's ok... I'm here. I'm not going anywhere," Tina said as she ran to her bedside. "Y'all go ahead. I'll stay with her."

"Tina, take this," Flea said. He pulled up his pants leg and pulled out a small .25 caliber pistol.

"What the hell am I gonna do with that?" Tina ask, showing him her chrome .45 with pink a grip handle. "I ain't got time to play with those niggas."

Tony smiled at the sight of the pistol he'd bought his sister. He knew from the first day he'd given it to her, she would always carry it. He looked at Flea as he looked at the gun in shock.

"When you get that, baby?"

"Let's just say, she's been around," she said as she gave her brother a wink. "Y'all go ahead. We're good."

"I love you, bae," Maine said, kissing Meka on the lips.

They left the hospital with one mission in mind. Killing Tweet and Zack. Tony, Maine and Flea drove through all the blocks.

"That nigga Tweet still in the hospital ain't he?" Maine asked.

"I don't know. Sarah only hit him in the shoulder. But you know L.G. He's got top notch security on him. We can't get to him right now."

"You right. But that nigga Zack out here somewhere," Flea said. *Bzzz-Bzzz-Bzzz.*

Tony looked down at the phone. It was Mindy. His heart began to speed up as he thought about what he had put her through.

"Hey baby," he answered. "I miss you."

"I miss you too. How's Sarah?"

"She's okay… she…"

"What baby? Talk to me."

"It's just a lot, Tony… She told me today that Tweet…"

"What! Where's he at! Is he there?" he asked, motioning for Maine to speed up.

"No Tony! No, he's not here… he's my brother."

"What!" Tony leaned back in the seat in disbelief, and became quiet as Mindy told him her mother's history with L.G.

"So this sick bastard didn't know he was about to rape his own sister?"

"Sister!" Maine and Flea said at the same time. Tony held up a finger for them to be quiet, so Mindy could finish her story.

"He don't know."

"Does L.G. know?"

"Yeah, but he's been paying my Mama to keep quiet about it."

"That's good to know, baby," Tony said as he began to put a plan together.

"How's that?" Mindy asked confused.

"Let's just say it's time we pay daddy a visit."

"You're crazy," she laughed.

"Crazy in love... with you."

* * * *

"How in the fuck you let that white bitch get off a shot?" Zack asked.

"Man, I'm telling you. The bitch creeped in my room on some Jason Voorhies type shit. All I heard was the bitch scream. Bro she was looking at me like she was lost or something. She just went to firing off shots. I'm glad her aim was off. I was dead. That nigga Tony had to knock her out to get the gun."

"You're kidding right?"

"No lie man, but fuck that – I'mma kill that bitch and her daughter."

"Well you know I paid that bitch Meka a visit." Zack said, eager to tell his story.

"Oh word?"

"I pissed all in her face then fucked that Ho ruff style."

"That's what I'm talking about," Tweet said, giving Zack a

pound with his left hand.

"So what's up with your pops?"

"Nigga on some fucking bullshit. He put his hands on me again. It's over. He's just another nigga to me. When I get back, I coming out with my own operation.

"Yeah. That's big shit."

"T.M.G..." Tweet said.

"Well you know I'm with you."

"What's up with the twins?"

"They're ready to party. Can you perform with one arm?" Zack said, giving his partner a playful jab.

"Shit... can Lebron come back from being down 3-1 and win a championship?"

"All. day."

"Well get those hoes on the phone and let's see what twin pussy feel like."

* * * *

L G. walked into Tess's office and stared at the empty seat. She had always been there to keep things in order. Boxes of money were stacked up on the floor waiting to be cleaned up. He walked behind the desk and sat down. Looking at her picture, he thought to himself, *please don't make me do this. I just need things to be the way they were.*" He opened the desk draw and began to pull out some papers, looking for the bank deposit invoices. L.G. noticed a file that read: "Tess private." He opened the folder and almost fainted. It was the documents of his drug organization along with the ten banks she used to clean his dirty money. "Why the hell would she keep a private folder of this?" He thought as he pulled out his phone.

"Hello. I guess you're ready to talk now, daddy?" Tess snapped before he could speak.

"What the fuck you got a private folder for?"

"Oh. That's nothing. Just the last ten years of your drug organization along with every dime you made and shipped out. By the way, that's your copy, I got it all on my flash drive. "

"What's gotten into you, Tess?"

"The same thing that's being going on with me for the last ten years, L.G. You! We made a baby, and guess what?"

"What?"

"You're gonna be a father, whether you like it or not!"

"Tess! Don't make me...."

"No mutha' fucka! Don't you make me!" She snapped back, ending the call.

L.G. slammed the desk drawer close. His whole organization was falling apart. He needed to get some things situated. Tess would be okay. He pulled out his phone and called Tony.

* * * * * * * * *

Tony, Maine and Flea were inside the jewelry store looking at rings. Tony picked up the Forever Us set by Jacob's Jewelry. A half-karat set that came with an engagement ring as well as his and hers wedding bands.

"What do you think about this?" Tony asked, holding up the jewelry box that came with a light that automatically came on when the lid was opened.

"Damn! How much?" Maine asked.

"Ten-five," Tony replied.

"She better say yes," Flea said, as he stared at the diamonds.

"She already has. I'll take this one in a size 5 ½." Tony said as he walked to the counter.

"I'm taking this one," Maine said.

"Man Flea, you better do something. Tina gonna be real pissed off if she's the only one not flossing," Tony said, counting out the money. "You know she got a new girlfriend with Pink trimming."

They all started laughing as Flea walked toward the glass casing that held the jewelry. As Tony waited for his future brother-in-law to pick out a ring, his phone vibrated.

"Yo, what's up?"

"This is L.G. Can we meet?"

"Time and place," Tony asked, nodding his head at Maine.

"How about my round table. It's a lot of issues I want to put to rest along with a proposal I have for you."

"For me?"

"Well let's just say, it'll be beneficial for *The Lick*." If I'm saying it correctly," L.G. said, letting him know that he was familiar with his crew.

"Time?"

"Four. Just pull up to the entrance gate, Oak will be waiting for you."

"We'll be there."

"Oh, Tony?"

"Yeah?"

"No Guns," L.G. said with a smirk.

"Of course not," Tony said as he felt the butt of his pistol in his waistline, ending the call.

After Flea picked out a two-karat chocolate diamond by Jacobs jewelry, they left the mall.

* * * *

Tweet and Zack were sitting in The House of Tekin with the twins when his phone went off. He looked at his father's number and was about to hit ignore, when Tamea gave him a look.

"Wifey?" she asked with a jealous look.

"Never that. Just business," he said, answering the call.

"What's up, Pops?"

"Be here at 4:00. No exceptions," L.G. said and ended the call.

Tweet looked down at his watch. It was 3 o'clock. "Zack, we. gotta be out bra."

"What the fuck's going on?" Zack asked, looking down at Tamia's body dress.

"Pops wants me at a meeting at four."

Zack knew that Tamia was gonna have to wait. Tweet and his father were not getting along, but Tweet wouldn't dare disrespect him by not showing up to a meeting. Looking at the sad look on Tamia's face, he did the only thing he could do to make-up. Zack pulled out a stack of bills and counted off fifteen one-hundred-dollar bills.

"Here baby. Go shopping while daddy make some more money."

"Okay," she said, giving him a passionate kiss.

"Let's go," Tweet said as he peeled Tamea off the same amount.

* * * *

Tony pulled up to the gate at exactly 3:45. He looked in his review mirror at the van that was following him. Oak stepped out of the security office to greet them.

"What's up, young blood?" He asked as he gave Tony a pound.

"They with you?" He continued, pointing at the white van following Tony's Audi.

"Yeah, just a little extra security."

"You don't need that. Everything's gonna be all good," Oak said as he pressed the security code. "Go to the guess house."

Tony and Maine pulled up to the guest house and got out. He waited for his guess to park, so they could enter together. He rubbed his waist to make sure his gun was tucked away.

The Lick

"Let's do this," Maine said, taking the steps two at a time.

They entered the guess house and were surprised at how it looked more like a huge office, rather than a house. The large cherry oak table surrounded by chairs took up most of the room. While they waited, Tess stepped out of her office to seat the guess. L.G. had begged her to come to the meeting. She sat in the office with her pistol stuffed in the back of her pants. She noticed the boxes of money had not been touched since the day she quit.

I'm not doing shit for him, she thought to herself as she looked across the room. Tess kept staring at the white women. She could not figure out how she played a part in all this. She turned her attention to the door as the Trap bosses entered the room.

Tweet and Zack pulled up to the guess house at exactly 3:55. He looked over at the Audi and point.

"I know that's not who I think it is."

"That look just like that nigga Tony's ride," Zack said, tucking his pistol.

"Can't be bra. That nigga ain't that stupid."

"Well, let's see," Zack said, exiting the Camaro.

They walked up the steps, passing the remainder of a blunt back and forth. Zack took a long pull before dropping it on the step and mashing it with the tip of his Timberland boot.

Wap', wap', wap!

Sounded the butt of the pistol as it slammed into Zack's face. "So you... *Wap!* want to... *Wap, wap!* Rape women, Nigga! *Wap, wap. Wap!*

Maine kicked Zack in the ribs, causing blood to pour from his face. Tweet pulled his pistol and aimed it at Maine heads.

"If you do, I'll raise your iron count to 100%," Tina said as she held her pistol steady.

"If he don't get off of 'em, he's a dead mutha' fucka!" Tweet shouted.

"That'll make two of y'all!" Tina snapped.

The Trap Bosses watched in amazement at the heart of the young crew. Tony pulled Maine off Zack as Tina kept her gun on Tweet.

"What the fuck is going on in here!?" L.G. asked, looking down at Zack.

"We're just getting to know one another," Maine said. "We got a lot of catching up to do," he continued, never taking his eyes off Zack.

"Well let's get down to business," L.G. said, taking a seat at the head of the table. "Order!" He called out as the room became completely silent. "We're here today to bring an end to the beef between my organization," he paused, "and *The Lick*."

Tweet stood by Zack as he stared at Tony and Maine. He looked around the room until he locked eyes with Mindy.

"What the fuck's going on?" he whispered to Zack, pointing at the back of the room.

"Tony, come forth," L.G. instructed. "Tell me. What must my organization do to bring a truce between the both of us, as well as get the documents to my business returned?"

"It's simple," Tony began as he turned to face Tweet and Zack. "You need to teach these two rapist mutha fucka's..."

"Watch your mouth..." Tweet snapped, as he jumped towards Tony.

"Stop!" Shouted L.G.

Tweet froze in place after hearing his father's voice. His eyes were locked on Tony with pure hate. He didn't give a damn what his father said. The only truces between them was gonna be when someone was rocked to sleep.

"As I was saying... keep these perverts at bay and kill any issues about the stash house we robbed."

"That's not a problem," L.G. said, walking over to shake Tony's hand.

"I'm not done," Tony said, pulling his hand back.

"As you know, me and my crew have developed a few Trap houses from the cocaine you allowed us to keep. We want to continue to work those blocks without the risk of turf wars from your Trap Bosses."

"I think I can make that happen," L.G. said, giving his Trap Bosses a quick nod. "Anything else?"

"I want you to supply *"The Lick"* with 100 kilos a month. The cash will be picked up every month by Oak when he makes his regular rounds."

"Fuck no!" Tweet screamed as he walked up to his father. "We will not help them eat. You told me that I was taking over the operation," he said, slamming his fist on his chest. "...And there's no way they're gonna eat off my table!"

L.G. looked at his son as he screamed in rage. He knew he could never be a leader. This organization made millions and took him all around the world. But just the short time his son had been in control, it had lost almost everything. In being a leader, L.G. knew what had to be done. He returned his sons stare.

"Rule number three?"

Tweet stood face to face with his father. With his fist clutched tight, he did not budge nor show an ounce of fear.

"Rule number three, Gotdammit!" L.G. snapped so close to Tweets face that spit flew onto it.

"I will not let the hate I have for my enemy," A female voice began as the faces in the room turned to find the voice. "Allow me to make a selfish decision that will cause the organization to suffer," Sarah said as she stood by Mindy.

It had been many years since she spoke those words. L.G. had made her learn them when they were together. Sarah stared into L.G.'s eyes with tears in her own. "Rule number five?" she asked him.

Tess stepped forward as this woman took the floor. She didn't know what the fuck was going on. But like every person in the room, she wanted to know.

"Rule number five!" Sarah screamed as she too pulled out a chrome .45 with pink grips.

Tony looked at the gun, then looked at Tina. "It's not mine," she whispered.

"Rule number five..." L.G. caused everyone to turn their heads back towards him. "Never put anything before family. When a choice must be made that involves family... always choose... blood."

Tears fell down Tess's faces as she listened to L.G. quote his own rules. She turned to walk into her office not able to take anymore. She took a step before the woman's next words crushed her soul.

"Well why did you do it?" Sarah asked, calmly causing the room that had grown to a small whisper to once again turn silent "Why did you leave us?"

"What are you talking about?" L.G. asked.

"You know what I'm talking about! Her!" Sarah said, pointing at Mindy who was now in tears. "Her, L.G.! Your daughter! I'm not hiding anymore!"

Tweet look at Sarah, then looked at his father. He needed this man to say something. Anything. His lifelong hero stood defeated. His mouth hung open as if he was in a daze. Tweet turned to Mindy. Could this be? Had he indeed tried to rape his own sister. He slowly walked towards his father. Out of the corner of his eye he saw Tess on her knees crying. What did she have to do with this? It didn't matter. The only answer he needed to know was in his face.

"Is it true?" he asked his father.

L.G. looked around the room. He hadn't noticed his wife Lisa standing in the doorway. She was now in tears with Sarah, Mindy and Tess. He couldn't run anymore. His money had kept his secret safe for years. But now it was out. All of it. He turned to Tess who was still on her knees in tears.

"It's true, Gotdammit... It's true!" He shouted.

Tweet turned and walked over to his mother. He whispered a few words, and she turned to leave. Stopping, she turned and walked over to L.G... and slapped him across the face without so much as a whisper. Satisfied for the moment, she turned and walked out. L.G. looked at Tony.

"Do we have a deal?"

"The documents will be delivered today. You have my word that nothing will be held, back."

They shook hands and L.G. walked toward Sarah. When he was face to face, he stopped and looked into her eyes, and she didn't budge or blink.

"Your daughter is over there," she said, pointing at Mindy.

L.G. walked towards Mindy. Without the first clue as to what to say, when he was face to face, he searched for the right words. When nothing came to mind, he simply stretched out his arms. Mindy walked into her father's arms. He wrapped his arms around her tightly and just held her close in a moment where no words were needed.

CHAPTER THIRTEEN

"Rise Up..."

Two weeks later, Maine walked into the hospital with a smile on his face. It was time to pick up Meka. He stopped by the hospital's floral boutique and picked up a huge white Teddy bear to go with his dozen white tip roses. As he stood on the elevator, butterflies ran through his stomach. The doors open and he looked down the hall at the small crowd. He walked up to Meka's father.

"How's everything going, Mr. Williams?" Maine extended his free hand.

"Call me Peter. And I'm fine. Listen, I would like to have a word with you, in private if you don't mind."

"Sure. One second," Maine said as he walked into the room. "For you," he gave Meka a quick kiss on the lips and handed her the gifts. "Be right back. "

"Where are you going?"

"Not too far," he said, stepping back into the hallway.

"What's up, Mr. Will... I mean Peter."

"Is it true that you know who did this shit to my daughter?" Peter asked once they were in private.

"Yes, I do, but trust me, this issue will get taken care of."

"That's not what I asked you. See player, I've been around a long time. Those same streets you're running now, I ran them a long time ago. And I left something back there that I'm not proud of. But I chose to change the game. And just because I changed the game, don't mean I forgot how to play. Now I need a name so I can pay this mutha fucka a visit.

"Mr. Peter, you don't..."

"Don't give me that!" He snapped. "I'm my own man. And trust when I tell you, I know the Demon of Death."

Maine looked into Peter's eyes, seeing a darkness he knew all too well. It was a darkness that would forever be there. Always in the shadow's waiting to be called upon. Never asleep and always available. He had the same look.

"Zack... Her ex-boyfriend," Maine said, knowing he had just given Zack a date with death.

"I never liked him anyway," Peter said as he walked away to join his family.

"What's going on?" Meka said, as she walked up to Maine.

Maine looked around at her father who had a smile on his face. It's was as if he had just hit the lottery. He turned his attention back to Meka.

"Nothing baby. I was just telling your father how I was the luckiest man alive to have you as my women. So, we had to debate the issue because he felt like he was the luckiest with your mother. After he told me how special she was today... after all the years they've been together, I can't wait to start our journey together."

"Okay, Maine. What are you saying?"

"Ms. Williams," Maine said as he got down on one knee and pulled a small black box out of his pocket. "I'm not saying anything. I'm asking... begging you... to be my wife," he continued, opening the box.

"Damn player!" Peter said, after his eyes landed on the ring. "What the hell you waiting on, girl?"

"Let her answer, Peter," Mrs. Williams said as she quickly compared the size of her daughter's ring to her own.

"Yes! Yes, Maine. Yes!" Meka screamed as she jumped into her father's arms.

"Hey! You're in the wrong arms. I didn't buy that ring."

"Not yet anyway," Mrs. Williams said, causing them all to start laughing.

* * * *

L.G. sat at the head of the table surrounded by his Trap bosses. The smile on his face let them know that business in the organization was back to normal. He stood up and walked to the middle of the floor.

"I want to thank all the Bosses for making it on such short notice.

I called everyone in today to let you know that with the addition of our new members, our numbers are up."

"Yeah. Yeah! Oooh, oooh..." cheered the group.

"Hold up. Hold up..." L.G. said, as he waved his hands to calm the group. "We're not completely out of the red yet. We still need someone to take over Rock's shipment. I've already purchased another warehouse. I just need another Boss."

"I'll take it," Flea offered as he raised his hand. "My block turned a quarter of the money your organization made these last two months. I can easily move my workers across the street in the warehouse you purchased. That would give me storage for more product and security."

"Security?" L.G. asked surprised at how Flea was revealing his new plans before they were spoken.

"Yeah, security. With my crew moving into the warehouse, it eliminates the robbers and the police. Giving me added protection I need to move more of your product."

"And how do you feel about this, Tony?"

"It sounds like a...."

"Well I don' like it!" Tweet snapped, cutting Tony off.

"You don't have a say," L.G. stated.

"And how's that? You turned the organization over to me. Remember?"

"And I took it back!" He said through clenched teeth. "The reign of the next Boss of this organization is now undecided. If you want it, you will have to prove yourself. With that being said, the new warehouse will be operated by 'The Lick'. "Let's make a toast!"

Tweet stared at his father as he sipped champagne from his crystal glass. He could not believe he was working with his enemy. But he had a plan that would open his father's eyes. He turned and walked out of the meeting before it was dismissed.

"Okay family, this meeting is over," L.G. said as he finished off his drink.

Tony waited until all the Trap Bosses had left before he walked towards L.G.

"Tony," L.G. said, extending his hand. When Tony approached, Flea was right behind him.

"I just needed a few minutes of your time before we leave."

"It's not a problem. What can I help you with?"

"Well I wanted to let you know that I'm about to marry Mindy, and I would like for you to be there."

"I'll be honored. And it'll be a privilege to handle the arrangements, if you would allow me to?"

"Thank you," Tony said.

"No, thank you. Tell my daughter that an unlimited Rush card is waiting for her."

"I'll let her know," Tony said, as him and Flea exited.

Tony pulled up to the security gate and waited for it to open. The meeting with L.G. was a success once again.

Bonk! Bonk! Tony pressed the horn for L.G.'s guard to let them out.

"What the fuck!" Flea said as he tried to look through the tinted glass. "Wait a minute," Flea said as he got out of the car and walked to the security door. "Hey!" Flea shouted, banging on the door. He turned the knob and the door opened with ease. "Excuse me, can you..." Flea stopped in mid-sentence after seeing the face behind the desk.

Tweet was sitting behind the desk with his pistol in full view. While talking on his phone, he gave Flea a sign to be quiet. Flea stood and listened as he macked to a female.

"Look man... just let us out!" Flea said, getting agitated. Tweet slammed the phone down as he looked up at Flea. "Don't you see a Boss talking?" he said as he placed his hands on his pistol.

"Just open the fucking gate!"

"And if I don't?" Tweet stared at Flea waiting for him to make his move. "I'm gonna tell you and your pussy ass partner for the last time. Y'all are on the wrong side of the fence. Now get the fuck out!" He shouted, pushing the button to open the gate.

Flea watched as Tony drove his Audi through the gate. When he was safely on the outside, he turned his attention back to Tweet.

"Hey, food for thought. You might just be on the wrong side of the fence." Flea gave Tweet a hard stare before walking out.

When he climbed into the car, Tony looked at him, "What took so long?"

"Just making sure we're on the right side of the fence," Flea said as he turned up Young Jeezy's hot single, *"Vacation!"*

* * * *

Tess stood in the mirror naked. She turned from side to side looking at her stomach. She was only two months pregnant but could see the changes her body had begun to take. Her nipples were swollen and tender to her touch. She could see her stomach had formed a small, soccer ball size knot. After finding out L.G. had a daughter, they had not spoken about their baby.

Sarah had gone to Atlanta to hide from L.G. when she was trying to keep her daughter safe. But Tess refused to be a prisoner in her own country. If L.G. didn't want to be a father to their child, that was his business. But he damn sure wasn't gonna make her kill it. He had called her not mentioning one word about her pregnancy. But she had a plan.

"Tess... I miss you," she thought replaying their conversation in her mind.

"What do you want L.G.," she recalled replying?

"We're having a meeting, and I need you there, Tess. Business has been good."

"L.G., you mean you need me to come in and clean up all the money and get it into the banks."

"Well, yeah, and...," L.G. stated.

"5%," Tess snapped.

"What!"

"You heard me. I want 5% of all the money I clean. I already have a new account set up that will deduct the money while it's being transferred."

"Tess, you don't have to do this. You know I will give you anything you ask for."

"Well, I take it we have a deal?"

"A deal?" L.G. asked.

"Yes. A business deal. One that won't involve sex. It's the only way that I will continue to work for you. Now do we have

a deal?"

"Yes. We have a deal," L.G. answered defeated.

Tess's plan was to get as much money out of L.G. as she could to take care of their child. But Tess still had another secret hidden in the walls of her heart. She was in love with L.G. He had been the only man that had touched her body since she came home from the navy ten years ago. Could she work around him and not allow her body to fall weak to his touch. "I have to for us," she said as she continued to look in the mirror. She took a shower, got dressed and headed for work. She took one last look in the mirror before heading to her office. With a new wardrobe that was less appealing, Tess still knew that she had a bigger problem. It was herself. She took a deep breath as she rubbed her stomach. "We can do this," she said to herself as she walked out the door.

* * * *

Zack laid back on the bed and squeezed his toes tight. As he watched Tamia swallow his ten-inch dick with no problem, she grabbed his balls and gently rubbed them with her free hand. During the dinner date, Tweet had secretly slipped E pills into the twin's drink.

"Damn, Ma!" Zack moaned as she fucked his dick with her mouth. "Oooh shit! Oooh shit!"

As Zacks climax intensified Tamia turned her body reverse, cowgirl style, giving Zack a full view of her caramel round ass. She reached between her legs and grabbed his dick, positioning it at the tip of her pussy. She slid down on it, inch by inch, allowing Zack to watch it disappeared. Tamia leaned forward and popped her hips as the sound of their bodies clapped. "Yes!!! Fuck me daddy! Fuck... me!" she screamed.

Zack rolled over and put Tamia on all fours. He could hear the bed banging against the wall next door as Tweet fucked the other twin. The sound of the screams excited Zack, and he pushed his dick back inside of Tamia with one thrust.

"Aaahh... wait! Wait!" she screamed from the pain. "Take it easy, baby."

Zack begin to fuck her with hard strokes. He sild his dick back, until it was almost free, and then forcefully slammed it back inside of her as far as he could."

"Oh my God! Tamia screamed. "I'm cumming, I'm cumming... I'm cummm...ing!!!"

Zack continued to fuck her long into the night. He would slow down, only to gain new stamina from the sounds of the headboards next door.

Two hours later, Tamia walked into the bathroom. Her body was sore from the rough sex. She sat on the toilet as she tried to replay what happened. Somewhere during their sexual encounter, things changed. She looked inside the toilet at the blood. She knew her insides had been damaged. She thought about her sister and ran out the bathroom. She began to get dress quickly.

"Hey what's up? I thought we would go for round four," Zack said, stroking his dick that was still rock hard from the ecstasy.

"My sister," Tamia mumbled as she ran next door.

She opened the door and her hands flew to her mouth as she let out a loud scream. "Aaaaahhh!!! Get the fuck off her!"

Tamea was unconscious, laying on her stomach with her head against the headboard as Tweet pumped into her dry insides from behind.

"I'm almost there," he grunted as he looked over his shoulder. "Shit... shit .. oooh shit, I'm nutting... I'm nutttiiinnn..." he moaned as he pushed deep into Tamea's lifeless body.

Tamia stormed over and pounded on Tweet with her fist. He

rolled off Tamea, grabbed his cloth's and walked out the door naked. When he was outside, Tamie secured the locks and ran over to Tamea.

"I'm sorry," Tamia said as she held her sister in her arms. "I'm so sorry."

Tamia dressed her sister as she continued to look over her body. She walked to the door, searching for Tweet and Zack. After scanning the parking lot, she saw that Tweet's Camaro was gone. Tamia grabbed her phone and dialed 911.

"Hello 911," the operator answered.

"Yes. I'm at the Red Roof Inn. Me and my sister have been sexually assaulted. She's unconscious and we need help immediately.

* * * *

"Put it down nigga!" Flea called out as he held the dice. "You need to drop another grand."

"I'm all in," said T.H., one of Flea's bodyguards.

Terrance "T.H." Lewis was young, wild and thuggin. His mother and father were crackheads. From the time he was born, he was introduced to the struggles of life. He became friends with Dirty Red and was taught the power of a pistol. It was Dirty Red that took Terrance on his first stick up. They were on the Southside in Macon, GA, watching a crew of Bloods serve fiends on the block. Terrence was hungry and broke, and Dirty Red promised him after tonight that hard living would be a thing of the past.

"It's six of them and only two of- us." Terrence said.

"Well that means we'll have to shoot three a piece," Dirty Red said as he continued to look down the block. "Check this out. See that girl sitting on the hood of the car across the street?" Dirty Red said.

"Yeah, Shorty tight work uh?"

"Go ask her for her phone number?"

"Fuck no! those nigga gonna kill me," Terrence said with fear in his eyes.

"Not if we kill them first. Now go!"

Terrence walked down the street with his heart about to jump out of his chest. Not only was he afraid to die, but he had never approached a female in his life. He looked down at the old Reebok Classic Dirty Red gave him over a year ago. *What am I supposed to say to her,* he thought as he approached the car? Terrence looked at the girl sitting on the car. She was the most beautiful woman he had ever seen in his life. He walked up to her and took a deep breath.

"Hey Sexy. Can I have your phone number?"

"Hey mutha' fucka!" A voice shouted. "That's my..."

Boom! Boom! Boom! sounded the pistol behind Terrence.

He pushed the girl to the ground before turning with his pistol raised.

Boom! Boom! Boom!

Terrence fired three shots, hitting three different targets.

He looked for Dirty Red who was chasing someone down the block.

Boom! Boom! Boom!

After Dirty Red cleaned out the guys pockets, he ran back up the block where Terrence was standing.

"Damn dog, you hit three of them. Where you learn to shoot like that?"

"Boy Scouts," Terrence answered truthfully.

"Triple Homicide on your first ride. You gotta street name bra!

T.H."

"T.H.?" Terrence repeated to himself.

"Bra, I'm taking you to my Boss."

"That's all you got!" Flea shouted as he switched the dice.

"Yeah, Now Roll a seven!"

"Minus one!" Flea said as the dice stopped on a pair of threes.

"Thank you, gentlemen, it's been a pleasure," Flea said as he picked up the money.

Flea and T.H. walked inside the warehouse. When they were alone in his office, he handed him all the money.

"Rule number two?" Flea asked with a smirk.

"I don't know Boss. Something about never that allows your enemies to make a decision that's too deep for your pockets."

"Hold on." *Beep-Beep...* "Daz! Step in my office."

Beep-Beep. "On my way, Boss." Flea's lieutenant responded.

"T.H. I want you to start saving all the money you can. You never know what the game's gonna throw at you. So, you must always be ready."

Knock-Knock.

"Come in!" Flea said as he watched T.H. grab his pistol, immediately changing from friend to bodyguard.

"You wanted to see me Boss?" Daz asked as he nervously looked at T.H.

"I just wanted to know how the product was moving."

"The weekly requirement was made as of today, we still got Thursday through Saturday which will be all profit for *The Lick.*"

"Good-Good. That's what I wanted to hear. Box up the money and have it ready for pick up at 6 o'clock."

"Boss, That's a lot of boxes. Can you give me until eight?"

"Eight? Daz, what's rule number six?"

"Never allow an excuse to be the reason for your failure," Daz said as he lowered his head. "It'll be ready at six, boss." Daz turned to leave as he said the rule again to himself. "Hey Boss?" he called out as he looked at his presidential Rolex.

"Yeah."

"Make it five."

"Now we're talking" Flea said as he called Tess to have the money picked up.

CHAPTER FOURTEEN

"Time up. . ."

Sarah sat on the couch inside *Brides To Be* and watched as Mindy tried on different dresses.

"What do you think about this one, Mama?" Mindy asked, turning towards her mother.

"Honey, it doesn't matter which dress you choose. You're gonna be a beautiful bride."

"Thanks Mama, but I want to look perfect" Mindy said, spinning back towards the mirror to look at herself.

"So which one will it be?" A voice asked from across the room.

Mindy and Sarah simultaneously looked across the room to find L.G. standing in the doorway of the store.

"How long have you been standing there?" Mindy asked, surprised.

"Long enough to know that Tony is one lucky man. That dress is perfect. We'll take it!" L.G. said to the Asian salesclerk. L.G. pulled out a platinum Visa and swiped it. After paying the $3500.00 tab for the dress, they walked out the store. "I need to talk to you." L.G. whispered in Mindy's ear. "Alone."

"You have my number, right?"

"Yes, but this can't be discussed over the phone. Let's do lunch today at noon. Meet me at Shane's Rib Shack in Statesboro."

"I can't eat there and fit in this dress," Mindy smiled, as she rubbed her belly.

"Well you'll just have to watch me eat," he said, laughing.

"I'll be there," Mindy hugged him before departing.

It was 11:45 and Mindy had finally convinced Sarah to let her go alone. She walked into the restaurant wearing a DKNY sweat suit. This was only lunch with her father, so she didn't want to over dress.

"Reservations for two at noon," she told the host.

"Name please?" The host with a German accent asked.

"Larry Goins."

"Ah yes, right this way, please," he said, giving Mindy a once over.

The host led Mindy to the back of the restaurant where L.G. was already seated and talking on his cellphone.

"Let me call you back," he said, ending the call.

L.G. stood and pulled out a chair for Mindy. After making sure she was comfortable, he sat down and handed her an oversized napkin.

"What's this for?" she asked with a puzzled look.

"Trust me. You're gonna need it."

"Are you ready to order, Mr. Goins?" The waiter called him by name.

"Yes, I'll have a rack of the houses Baby Back Ribs, well done, with Sweet Baby Ray Barbeque Sauce."

"And your drink?"

"I'll have a glass of Ciroc with a dash of honey. Leave it at room temperature, please."

"And your lady friend?"

"My daughter," L.G. corrected.

"I'm sorry, sir. What will your daughter have?"

"This is her first visit here," he informed the waiter. "Allow me to order for you?" he suggested after turning his attention to Mindy.

"Okay," she said surprised. "But don't overdo it."

"For her, bring the Mrs. Ribs platter. Well-done of course, but for her add the sweet and sour honey barbeque sauce."

"And her drink?"

"Long Island Ice-tea." Mindy interrupted.

"Be back in a few," the waiter said, turning to walk away.

"Oh, so you're a regular here, I see."

"Yeah, one of my favorite spots."

"Cool! So what did I do to deserve lunch with you?" Mindy asked.

"Nothing. It's just somethings I need to take care of that is long overdue. I wanted to spend some time with you and get to know you better."

"That's good to hear. Now cut the B.S. and give it to me straight. "

L.G. looked at his daughter. He saw that she was not the naive little girl her looks portrayed. She had his blood, so he knew she was too smart for him to manipulate with words. So if he wanted his plan to work, he definitely needed her on board.

"Listen Mindy," he began. "I know you and Tony are about to get married, so I want to make sure you are well taken care of. I am trying to retire from the game and Maurice just ain't ready to take over. So I want Tony to run the organization."

"You mean you want him to run your drug business!" She snapped.

"Don't look at it like that. This is an opportunity most people would kill for."

"Or get killed doing!" She abruptly said. "No! I won't allow it.

Tony's not that type of guy," she said, attempting to get up.

L.G. rushed around the table and placed his hands on her shoulders, stopping her from leaving.

"Are you blind, Mindy? Where do you think all that nice shit he owns is coming from? The houses, the cars – Hell, and most of the shit he buys you?"

Mindy looked at her father with a sad defeated look. She knew that Tony had come up overnight. And he damn sure wasn't pulling no 9-5 job. Her attention was broken when the waitress returned with their food.

"Will there be anything else?" she asked, carefully placing their food on the table.

"No. Thank you very much," L.G. said without taking his eyes off Mindy.

"Well enjoy," she said, walking off.

"You're gonna love this," L.G. said as he leaned over and savored the sweet aroma of the smoked ribs.

"Smells good," Mindy said as she gave him a cold stare.

"Taste it."

"I'm not hungry," Mindy replied as she got up to leave.

"Let's talk about this like adults."

"What's there to talk about? You taking the only man I have ever loved."

"Mindy!" L.G. shouted as he watched her storm out of the restaurant.

* * * *

Tony was at the carwash waiting on the finishing touches to be done to his Audi. He felt the vibration of his phone and looked down at his soon to be wife's face.

"Hello love of my life," he answered.

"And congratulations to you too," Mindy shot back.

"For what?"

"For becoming my.... my whatever the hell you want to call him, drug Boss."

"What sweetheart? What on earth are you talking about?"

"What am I talking about? No Tony... it's what you need to be talking about. I just left my father and he has plans of turning his business over to you. My future husband. So I asked him why do you always take the people I love?"

Tony was in shock. This was news to him. As Mindy continued to vent her frustrations, Tony's phone began to flash, signaling an incoming call was in process. He looked at the name and saw that it was L. G.

"And Tony, I don't like it!" Mindy continued, "Please tell me… no, promise me you won't do it. Promise me, Tony."

"Listen Mindy. I don't even know what's going on. Let me take this call and we will discuss it later."

"Alright," Mindy said, feeling as if she had convinced him.

"What's up?" Tony said, clicking over to L.G.

"Tony… Tony... Tony. How are you doing my soon to be son-in-law?"

"Well I won't speak too soon on that after the lunch you had with Mindy. I've been on the phone with her, she told me your plans."

"And they were?"

"To run your organization. What about Tweet. He's your son... your blood. He'll never stand for me sitting at the top of his throne."

"See Tony, that's where your wrong. It's my throne, and I'll sit the best person for the Job on it. Right now, I believe that it's you. I gave my son a chance, and I lost a lot of money. But you and your crew have made me more money in the past three months than all my trap bosses combined. And I know it all comes from your leadership. That's why I'm offering you a seat at the top of the throne. Don't worry about Mindy. She loves you son; she will not stay mad for long. A couple of trips across the country and she'll forget how to be upset all together."

"I don't know, L.G."

"Of course you know.... The meeting is tonight at 6 o'clock, be there. I'll make the announcement then." L.G. said, ending the call.

Tony stood in the middle of the carwash parking lot in a daze. He couldn't believe this was happening. After another fifteen minutes of thinking, his car was ready. He paid for the services and pulled off with one person on his mind, Maine.

"What's up, my G." Maine answered.

"I gotta phone call from L.G."

"What's up? Everything's good, right? We kept our end of the deal and were making him hella rich. What did he want?"

"He wants me to run the whole organization."

"What the Fuck!!! You're kidding me, right?"

"No jokes here, and he has a meeting set for six to make the announcement to all the Trap Bosses."

"Today! Damn G. what are you gonna do?"

"It don't look like I have a choice."

"What did Mindy have to say about this?"

"She's the one who broke the news. L.G. talked to her first."

"Damn! Well I'm happy for you, now we'll see more money than ever before."

"Yeah, but at what cost?" Tony asked still confused.

"At a boss cost. Now let's get this money. If they ain't with us, then they against us. I'll see you at six, G." Maine said, ending the call.

Tony looked at his watch. It was 5 o'clock. He could feel sweat form on his forehead. He closed his eyes, stopping at a red light.

Bonk!!! Sounded a horn behind him, drawing Tony's attention to his rearview mirror as the driver flipped him off.

Without responding, he smashed the gas leaving his newfound enemy behind. Tony picked up his phone and called Mindy.

"Where are you?" she immediately asked.

"I'm driving down Claxton Dairy Road."

"You're gonna take the position, ain't you?"

"I have to."

"No, you don't have to. Just say that you want to."

"I do. But I want you by my side. I want to know that through all the good and the bad, you're with me."

"Tony, I'll always be there for you. I just want what's best for our family."

"We'll be fine, sweetheart. You have to trust me."

"I hope so," Mindy said defeated.

"I know so," Tony replied, knowing she was down with him.

* * * *

Tess was laying across her bed watching her daytime soap operas when an emergency all-points bulletin came across the screen.

Reporter:

"This is Molly Davis with breaking news. An A.P.B. has been issued for the arrests of Maurice Goins, AKA Tweet, and Zachery Brown, who goes by the street name –Zach. State officials said the warrants for the arrests of these two suspects stem from the alleged Date Raped of two sisters. The suspects were accused of putting drugs in the sister's drinks. The police reports suggest that after drugging the victims, the suspects took them to a nearby hotel and sexually assaulted them. The names of the sisters have not been released, due to the ongoing investigation. As soon as new information is released, we will keep you updated. This is Molly Davis with breaking news."

Tess stared at Tweet and Zack's face, as their images appeared to be frozen on the television screen. Shocked, she immediately grabbed her phone and called L.G.

"Hello," L.G. answered. "I'm glad you called. We have a meeting at 6 o'clock, I need everyone there."

"You might be minus one. Turn to Channel 6 and see if you can catch the Breaking News Report in five minutes."

"What is it?" L.G. said, picking up the remote.

"It's your son."

"What the fuck has that boy done now?"

L.G. watched the blond hair white woman as she made his son look like a wild animal on the loose. He immediately began to put his plan into action as Tess's voice broke his thoughts.

"Are you still there?" she asked.

"Stupid Mutha Fucka?" L.G. shouted into the receiver. "Let me call you later," he ended the call.

He rewound and replayed the news one last time. Frustrated, he called Oak.

"What's up, Boss?" Oak answered.

"I just saw my son on the news. Have you heard anything in the streets?"

"Yeah Boss. It's floating around heavy. Word is, Tweet and Zack put something in these twins' drinks, and then took them to a hotel. Word is, it got really rough. They said the one raped by Tweet had to have stitches. I heard he tore her insides up pretty bad. I got a guy watching their house right now, Boss. Do you want me to silence the witnesses?"

"No, not yet. Just get them to me right now."

"We're on the way," Oak said, ending the call.

* * * *

Tweet pulled up to the gate and pressed the visitor's button. He looked over at Zack. After hearing that his father had a mandatory meeting at 6 to announce Tony as the head of the organization, he was done. He wanted nothing to do with his father's organization any longer, and he was doing the only things that made sense. Starting on his own.

"State your name and business," a husky voice muffled through the intercom.

"This is Tweet. L.G.'s son. Let me in."

Crop was an old school hustler. He had retired years ago after taking a bullet for his longtime friend and business associate L.G. Crop had made millions throughout the years with L.G. But his street run came to an end when a group of thugs attempted to rob his crew. Oak shot first hitting one of the robbers. But as he fired off a shot he was hit as a shot was fired at L.G. Crop took the bullet that would later prove to cripple him for life. Less than 60% with his movements, he called it quits and begun to enjoy the fruit of his labor.

"What can I do for you young fellow?"

"I need to talk to you, open up."

The huge gate opened, and Tweet made his way to the front of Crop's mansion. Crop was already out-front waiting when they arrived.

"What's up old timer?" Tweet said as he and Zack got out.

"Nothing much just enjoying life. How's your father?"

"He's alright, I guess. Just being him. Look I need your help.

Let's go inside and talk," Tweet said heading toward the double glass doors with gold trimmings.

They went inside and Crop listened as Tweet got straight to the point. He displayed a drive and ambition Crop had only seen in one other man, L.G.

"Crop I need you to supply me."

"What about your father, son?"

"I'm not worried about him. I'm my own man and I want to handle my own business. Now, we can start with 250-kilos. I'll open three trap houses the first week. After that, I'll open three more. I'll make you rich Crop."

"I'm already rich, son."

"Well, you can help make me rich. I won't let you down, Crop, just give me a chance."

Crop thought about the first night he met L.G. He was broke and homeless, and he begged L.G. for a chance to make money with him. They became close friends and later became millionaires together.

"Son, give me a day or two to think about it. I'll give you a call with my answer."

"Crop, I need you to..." Tweet began as his phone went off.

He looked down at his father's name and pressed the ignore button.

"You might want to answer that," Crop said, looking at Tweet with a serious look on his face.

"It's not important. What's important is you telling me that you will get me the product I need."

"Like I said to you earlier, I will get back with you. Now leave. I must get my rest."

"I'll be waiting for your call," Tweet advised, as he turned to leave with Zack following close behind.

CHAPTER FIFTEEN
"Making Money…"

As Oak pulled through the gate, he looked in the rearview mirror at the girls in the back seat.

"We're almost there," he said, heading toward the east wing of L.G.'s mansion.

"Where are you taking us?" Tamia asked afraid.

"Listen to me ladies. This situation could end very good or very bad for the both of you. So think before you speak, make the right choice, and you'll have nothing to worry about. Understand?"

"Then why are we handcuffed and blindfolded?" Tamia asked.

"For your safety. We're here now. Let's take care of business," Oak said, getting out to open the sliding door. "Easy now, watch your step," he continued as he helped the twins.

"Where are we?"

"Take my hand and follow my instructions," Oak said as he stood between the girls.

Giving each one of his hands, Oak led the girls to a large room where L.G. was already waiting.

"Take the cuffs and blind folds off," L.G. said, as he poured himself a drink.

L.G. stood back and watched the girls take in the massive room. Tamia walked over to the window. The huge lawn and swimming pools below told her that this situation was serious.

"Why are we here?" she asked, turning back to L.G.

"Are you gonna kill us?" Tamea asked.

"No, I don't want to hurt you. However, we have business that we need to take care of."

"What kind of business?" Tamia asked.

L.G. took out his phone and placed it on the table. "This business," he said, as pointed to a picture of Tweet.

"That's him!" Tamea screamed as she stared at Tweet like she'd seen a ghost. "He raped me."

"This is my son."

"Your son!?" Tamea asked surprised.

"Yes. And I'm here to make you an offer to settle this once and for all.

"Settle it how? The cops are looking for him and his friend."

"You don't worry about the cops. I'll handle them. Do you have family outside of Georgia?"

"Yes, in Florida," Tamea answered.

"What part?"

"Winter Haven. You may know our uncle, Pistol," Tamea suggested, knowing L.G. would know a known killer.

"I've heard of him," L.G. said already aware of their entire family; especially Pistol. "But here's my offer. I have $250,000 cash for each of you, along with a place to stay and transportation. All you have to do is leave Georgia and don't return."

"And if we return?" Tamia asked.

"Then you will leave me no choice," L.G. said with a serious look on his face.

"Choice on what?" Tamia asked confused.

"We'll leave town," Tamea said.

"Good answer. Oak...?"

"Yeah Boss?"

"Get these girls their money and give them their new address. Oh, and call Pistol and let him know that they're on the next flight out of Georgia."

"Got it Boss. By the way, it's 6 o'clock. The Trap Bosses and 'The Lick' are waiting on the west wing for you."

"Time flys," L.G. said as he looked at his watch. "Well ladies it's been a pleasure. Spend your money wisely," he advised as he walked out the door.

As L.G. walked out, he noticed the window at the security gate and then saw an unmarked police car that was being followed by a Lauren's County Sheriff Deputy. He picked up his phone and called Tess.

"Yes," she answered.

"Let the guys know that I'm gonna be a few minutes late."

"Alright?"

L.G. walked outside and climbed on a golf cart. He drove up to the gate where his unwanted guests were waiting.

"They wanted me to open the gate, Boss. They said something about a warrant for your son." The security guard said. "But I didn't let them in," he continued, knowing had he let the police in, he would have signed his own death certificates.

"Good job," L.G. said, walking up to the unmark car. "Why are you on my property?"

"I have a warrant for the arrest of a Maurice Goines, aka Tweet. Last known address is listed as the Goines Estate," The stubbed bearded, white headed officer said.

"What's it for?"

"One count of sexual assault and one count of rape."

"Listen Officer..."

"Phillips..." the officer corrected him.

"Okay, Office Phillips. If my son did this horrific crime, then I want to make sure justice is served. Do you have any witnesses?"

"Yes, I have the victims themselves," Phillips assured him.

"Then let's sit down. You with your attorney and the witnesses, and I'll have my son as well as our family attorney accompany us. Then we'll find out exactly what took place, because from what my son says, it was consensual sex. And we both know how kids are."

"That's fine, Mr. Goines. Meet me at 8 a.m. at the courthouse."

"We'll be there. Good day," L.G. said, climbing back on the golf cart to drive towards the west wing. L.G. thought about his son's action and knew that he was about to make the right decision. He walked into the room and his presence alone caused the room to grow silent.

"Sorry I'm late," L.G. said, looking around to greet people in the room. He stepped into Tess's office. "No word from my son yet, huh?"

"No, I haven't seen nor heard anything from him."

"That figures," L.G. said as he pulled out his phone and called him again.

Tweet looked at his father's call and was about to press the ignore button, when Zack spoke up.

"It might be an emergency, homie. Just hear him out. If he's on the same bullshit, send him to voice mail."

"I ain't trying to hear shit he got to say, when Crop calls back tomorrow, we good."

"And if he don't?"

"He will. A true hustler will never turn down a chance to make a bank roll."

"I hope you're right," Zack said, watching Tweet press ignore. "Bra', have I failed you yet?"

"No, but..."

"No buts. I got this!!" Tweet said as his phone went off again. "The old man just won't...shit it's Tess!"

"Tess? What the fuck she calling for?"

"I don't know but we'll definitely need her to clean this money for us."

"That Bitch gonna tell your pops."

"Not if we make it worth her while," Tweet said as he held up a finger to silence Zack. Immediately, he called her.

"What's up, Tess?" Tweet said in a relaxed tone.

"There's a meeting about to take place, and you might want to be here."

"Nah... I don't need to be there. My pops got his head so far up Tony's ass now, he don't even have time to put it in yours anymore.

"Whatever. Just get your ass here ASAP."

"I'm good. Let him turn everything over to Tony."

"While you all worried about Tony, you might want to catch the cities breaking news."

"Why? What the fuck does the daily news have to do with me?"

"Everything! Now get your ass out of the streets before you go to jail."

"I'm good. Listen we need to talk."

"What can me and you possibly have to talk about?"

"Making money."

"Get here now!" Tess said, ending the call.

Tweet downloaded the "Breaking News" and was shocked when he saw the pictures of his face as well as Zack's from their High School yearbook on the screen.

"What the fuck," Tweet mumbled as he passed his cellphone to Zack.

"Oh shit! Those hoes went to the police," Zack said afraid.

"We got warrants. We gotta get out of this car."

"Let's go to the meeting. Then we can get your pops to help us."

"Fuck no!" Tweet snapped. "We don't need him. All we gotta do is take care of the twins. No witnesses. No case."

"Man, I don't know."

"Don't panic on me... we're gonna get rid of this car then take care of those hoes."

Tweet parked the car at Fairview Park Hospital. He walked into Enterprise Rental with a fake I.D. and they left with a Nissan Titan truck.

"Let's take care of this, then we'll go to the meeting. It'll be the perfect alibi," Tweet said as he headed towards the twins house.

Thirty minutes later, Tweet and Zack pulled up in Cascade Plaza. Tweet rode passed the twins house to find it dark and quiet.

"Those hoes are sleep. Just like we're gonna leave them," Tweet said, making a U-turn at the end of the block.

Tweet parked the truck on the corner and the two walked up the street like it was their home. They walked to the back of the twins' house and begin to look through the windows.

"Let's go in. They got to be in there."

"Yeah," Zack said.

"Both cars are in the garage." Tweet walked to the door and noticed it was cracked. "It's already open."

"Shhhh... I hear music," Zack said, making their way inside.

Tweet and Zack put on their ski-masks and walked down the hallway with their pistols out. When they made it to the bedroom door, Tweet could hear the music. Without wasting any time, he rushed into the room.

"What the fuck!" Zack said, entering the empty room.

Clothes were all over the bed and the floor as if a tornado had been through there.

"They gotta be close, check the rest of the house," Tweet ordered.

After searching the bedroom closets, Tweet and Zack headed out of the house. While walking through the kitchen, a phone went off.

"That's you," Tweet said, looking down at his phone.

Zack pulled out his Galaxy. "Nah Homie. Over there," he said pointing at the counter.

Tweet walked to the kitchen counter and picked up the pink iPhone. "36 missed calls. Damn... That bitch gotta hotline," Zack said. "That... or, more than us are looking for them."

"Bra, those hoes hiding out in witness protection. I'm willing to bet my last. The police got them hiding out to come to court and testify against us.

"Don't panic, man. We don't know that yet."

"That's why we need to go see your pops. He's the only one that can fix this. Man, we're the Breaking News headline. This shit done got real."

"I don't need his help!! And I ain't going to no fucking meeting to watch my fuckin' old man give our family's organization to another mutha' fucka. Now you can chill with that shit."

"Those crackers down at that courthouse gonna bury us. Watch and see. We gotta go see him. We have to! Do you want to spend the rest of your life in prison? If not, then you better get your head in the game. If Crop calls with the supply for us, how are we gonna take over the streets with the cops looking for us?"

"I'll figure it out," Tweet said, knowing his best friend was right.

"It's already figured out," Zack said, walking out of the twins' house. "We're going to this meeting."

"Fuck it, we'll go!! But I ain't got shit to say to Tony. And if that mutha fucka so much as looks at me, I'm putting two to his dome. No questions!"

"Cool," Zack said, relieved that he at least now had him heading in the right direction. "We go to the meeting. Let your pops have his moment, then we talk to him about this situation we're in. Alone."

"Alright. Let's go," Tweet said as they climbed into the truck.

* * * *

L.G. walked out of Tess's office and immediately began to look around the room for Oak. When they made eye contact, he gave a head nod for him to come talk to him in private.

"What's up, Boss?" Oak whispered, turning his back to the table.

"Is that business done?"

"It's done. They were flying Delta's friendly skies 30 minutes after we left. First class at that."

"Good job. Now let's get this meeting started." L.G. turned back to his Trap bosses. "Good evening, gentleman. Oh, and ladies," he said, making eye contact with Tess. "I brought you all in because there's gonna be some immediate changes."

"I thought you said our numbers were up?" One of the Trap bosses asked.

"They are. The numbers are great," L.G. said, walking towards Tony.

"Tony," L.G. said with his hand extended.

"What's up, Boss?"

"You don't ever have to call me Boss. Matter of fact, you're in the wrong seat. I need you to take the seat at the head of the table," L.G. said, pointing at his former seat.

Tony got up and walked to the Bosses chair. He looked down the table at all the Trap Bosses who would now not only rely – but depend on him as well. He felt a wave of butterflies in his stomach and was about to let L.G. know that he would decline his offer when his thoughts were broken by an opening door.

He looked towards the noise and saw Tweet and Zack walk in. Instead of sitting at the table, they took seats in the back of the room.

"Don't mind us," Tweet said, pulling out his cellphone. "I'm sure pretty boy phony Tony has a lot to talk about!"

Tony stared at Tweet and was about to respond to his comment when he thought of the greatest form of retaliation.

"As a matter of fact, I do have somethings to talk about. L.G. has given me the privilege of taking over this organization, and I want to make sure I don't fail like his piece of shit son."

"What Mutha Fucka!" Tweet said, jumping up to pull out his pistol.

Before he could lift his arm, every Trap boss in the room; including Oak had weapons pointed at him and Zack. Nobody spoke a word, as each awaited instructions from their new boss.

"Do we have a problem?" Tony asked, looking from Tweet to Zack.

"We good," Zack said, motioning for Tweet to sit back down.

"As I was saying," Tony said, turning his attention back to the table, "I've been given a very large honor. And I will not fail. I will not fail because you will not fail. We are a team as well as family. I've been placed in this seat, but I know and understand that without you... this seat is worthless."

"Speak! Young wise man," Oak said, winking at L.G.

"I can do nothing by myself. But as one, we can rise to great heights. As of today, every Trap Boss will receive 250 extra kilos a month. These 250 kilos(only), will be $1,000.00 cheaper, this alone will guarantee every Trap Boss a quarter million dollars every month to live on."

"Yeah ..." clapped all the Bosses...

Tony looked at L.G. The plan had worked. They accepted him

as their boss with opened arms. With that, L.G. knew they would not only be loyal, but they would protect him at all cost.

"We will function as normal, with only one change. Flea will now work hand-in-hand with Oak as First Lieutenants, along with Maine as well. These three men will be your contacts to get resupplied. And as a token of my appreciation to you for accepting me, I would like to give you these."

Flea opened a suitcase and began to pull out 22" platinum chains with a, *"The Lick"* encrusted diamond medallion for each Trap Bosses. He placed the final two chains around the necks of L.G. and Oak.

Tony personally walked over to Tess and gave her a chain that was chocolate brown with the same, *"The Lick"* medallion. Her crystals were pink and blue.

"Of course, we can't forget the true brains of the operation," he said. "Look the agreement between you and L.G. has been brought to my attention. I would like to ask you to stay as my accountant, but one thing has to change."

"And what's that?" Tess asked confused, yet serious.

"The five percent."

"What about it? It's that or nothing," she firmly said.

"You'll get 10 percent of all money you touch, as well as new electronic money counters. Nothing will be spared to keep the First Lady happy. That is... if you'll stay of course."

"I like you already," Tess said, placing the chain around her neck.

"Well I think I've covered everything. I want to thank you all for coming out. I look forward to working with each of you. Oh, and before I forget, the monthly meeting to discuss profits and losses will continue. Anything else?" Tony asked, directing his attention to L.G.

"Tony, you left nothing uncovered, so I don't have anything to say. Job well done. It's your team, dismiss at will."

"You all may go," Tony said, walking up to a few of the Trap Bosses to shake hands.

Tony looked towards Tweet and Zack who were still in the back staring at him through hate filled eyes. After his business was done, he walked out with Flea and Maine by his side.

"I wanted those niggas to try something," Maine said, climbing into the van.

"The picture has just gotten bigger, Bra. We have to beat them with our brains," Flea said, looking over at Maine.

"He's right. The stakes are too high. And at the end we must always be on top," Tony said as he pulled through the security get.

* * * *

L.G. continued to sit at the table with his back to Tweet and Zack. He interlocked his fingers. Placing his hands behind his head, he leaned back in the chair and spoke, "I'm waiting."

"I need to talk to you. I was just letting your new successor sink into your mind," Tweet said, being sarcastic.

"It don't have to sink in. I think it was the right decision."

"How? I'm your son!"

"Without the first ounce of stability!" L.G. said, standing up to face his son. "You're out of control!"

Tweet stood up and walked towards his father. The last thing he wanted to do was piss him off.

"I need... well we need your help."

"It figures."

"We have warrants, and now the police are looking for us. As soon as they locate us, we're getting locked up."

"For what?" L.G. asked as if he had not the first clue as to what his son was talking about.

"They trying to say we raped some girls. But it was all consensual. We went out to eat and then went to the hotel," he lied.

"Well why would a warrant be out for your arrest?"

"I don't know. Can you help us?"

"I'll make some calls, and we'll go down to the courthouse in the morning. Just stay under the radar until then."

"Thanks pop," Tweet said, feeling a big burden lifted off his shoulders. He turned to Zack and motioned towards the door. "Let's go. We should be good," he whispered as they headed out of the room.

CHAPTER SIXTEEN

"Gotcha…"

Mindy was laying on the bed with tear filled eyes. She could not believe she had agreed to support Tony as he ran her father's business. She rubbed the small mound on her stomach. After taking a pregnancy test almost a week earlier, Mindy now knew that she was carrying Tony's child. She had not told anyone about the baby; not even her mother. As she thought about her future and the future of her unborn child, her phone went off.

"Yes," Mindy said as she looked at Meka's face on the screen."

"Damn Bitch! That don't sound like the voice of someone who is about to get married. Shit, I can't wait to have some live-in dick."

"You're crazy," Mindy said, letting a small smile escape.

"Shit watch and see how I do it. I'll be riding that good dick all night and spending his money during the day," Meka continued to talk.

After a few minutes, she noticed her BFF was quiet again.

"Okay Bitch… spill it," Meka said with a serious tone.

"Tony…"

"What about him?"

"He's taking over my father's business."

"Your joking! I thought he gave it to that piece of shit son of his. "

"He did...but after the business lost a lot of money, he took it back. He took me out to eat and prewarned me."

"And you agreed?"

"Not with him... but after telling Tony that I really didn't like the idea I told him that I would be by his side."

"And that's where you're supposed to be. I'll ride with Maine to hell if he needs me to. We real bitches... now pull yourself together... we're Queenpins now."

"Queenpins?"

"Yeah... Drug Kingpins wives."

"But that's not it," Mindy said lowering her voice in case her mother was snooping outside her door.

"Okay what else bitch? You're not gonna tell me you found another brother, right?"

"No nothing like that."

"Well spit it out. Damn you gonna make a bitch play jeopardy."

"I'm preg..."

"You what?"

"I'm pregnant," Mindy whispered into her phone.

"Bitch I'm on my way," Meka said as she ended the call.

Ten minutes later Meka was in downtown Dublin waiting for a light to change. She looked in her rearview mirror and saw a black truck very close behind her. She let her Camry roll forward putting space between her and the truck only to find it returning.

"Stupid!" she shouted out her window.

When the light turned green Meka mashed on the gas pulling away from the truck. She stopped at the next light and this time the truck pulled beside her. She looked over at the truck as the tinted passenger window began to lower. Meka looked into Zack's face and fear gripped her heart.

"Oh shit!" she said as she looked up at the light, "I can't stay here."

Meka pressed her horn getting the attention of other drivers as she pulled her car out into traffic.

Booommmp!! screamed the horn of a car barely missing her front fender.

Meka turned into the flowing traffic and pressed the gas. She had just cheated death. She picked up her phone and called her father.

"Daddy! Daddy! He's behind me. He's following me," she screamed into the phone.

"Who!!? Who's following you!?"

"Zack! he's in a black truck!"

"Okay where are you now?" her father asked, putting his plan into action.

"I'm headed toward East Dublin. Daddy, hurry!"

"Listen to me, I'm gonna need you to calm down. Now have you called anybody else?"

"No just you. Daddy I'm so scared."

"Okay good. I promise you have nothing to worry about.
Now do you know where Miller's Country Club Road is?"

"I'm almost there now."

"Good. I need you to take that road until you get to the old airport."

"Why? I'm going all the way into nowhere. He's gonna kill me."

"You'll be fine. Trust me. Now turn on the maintenance road beside the airstrip."

"I'm almost at the maintenance road now."

"Is the truck still in sight?"

"Yeah. It's speeding up now."

"Ok. Just drive normal. Are you on the back road yet?"

"Turning now."

"Okay. This is very important. So follow my instructions carefully. Do you understand?"

"Yes."

"Okay stop."

"What! "

"Stop the car!"

Meka stop the car and watched in her rearview as the truck turned in behind her.

"Now get out."

"Please daddy! I'm scared!" Meka screamed into the phone crying through tears.

"Get out the car."

Meka slowly opened the car door. She climbed out of the car barely able to stand on her shaking legs. Placing her phone on top of the car she waited for her father's next instructions through the voice speaker.

Zack jumped out of the truck before it made a complete stop. Storming towards Meka he strapped on a pair of leather gloves.

"You think this a mutha' fuckin game!"

"Oh God!" Meka screamed as he got closer.

Three steps away Zack froze in his steps as the first shot pierced his side.

"Pop-pop," sounded the gun as two more bullets knocked him off his feet.

"Go home now!" shouted the voice through her phone.

Meka climbed in her car and sped away leaving Zack and the black truck behind.

Tweet ran to his friend's side. With his gun out he looked around searching for the shooter.

"You're gonna be ok."

"I don't know. They got me good."

"It's not that bad. Come on get up. We gotta get you to the hospital."

"Uuughh !!"

"I know the feeling. Now dammit push your legs."

Tweet got Zack off the ground and pushed him into the back seat of the truck. He smashed the gas as he fought against time. Zack was losing blood fast.

"Talk to me partner."

"I'm sleepy man."

"No, you gotta stay up!" Tweet screamed as he took out his phone and pressed 911.

"My friend has been shot. I'm on my way to Fairview Park hospital. Can you please have someone waiting for us.?"

"Is he still breathing?"

"Yes. But he's losing blood fast please just have someone at the door in five minutes." Tweet said as he ended the call.

"Hang in there homie. We're almost there."

"Damn, this shit hurt like a mutha' fucka. That bitch set me up."

"Don't worry about her. She'll pay with the rest of them. Just breathe.

Tweet pulled into the parking lot. Lights were flashing at the emergency entrance. Doctors and Nurses were waiting as he slammed on his brakes at the doors.

"He's in the back! Tweet shouted as he climbed across the seat.

"Oh, my Lord. What happened to him?" The doctor asked as he lifted Zack's shirt.

* * * * * * * * *

Meka walked into her house with tears in her eyes. Her father was sitting at the kitchen table with a cup of coffee between his fingers.

"Are you okay?" he asked in a low tone.

"Is he dead?" she asked as she nodded her head up and down.

"That's not my concern. He touched something of mine, so he created a debt. And debts must be paid. Now listen to me. Go take a shower, lay down and rest. When you wake up this will be a thing of the past. And we're to never speak of it again. Not even to each other. We carry it to our graves. Do I make myself clear?"

"Yes daddy," Meka said as she walked away.

CHAPTER 17

"Trap Doing Good..."

"How much is that?" Flea asked as he watched his crew stuff the last bag of money into the van.

"That's two mill," Daz said as he closed the door. "Alright T.H., take it to Tess. Remember drive the speed limit.

"I got this. You must think this my first time," the wild one said as he started the engine.

"It must be. Now fasten your seat belt," Daz joked.

Since the death of Dirty Red, Flea had vowed to take care of T.H. Young, wild and with a quick temper, the job was never easy.

"Where's your gun T.H.?" Flea asked.

"Dam!" He said as he pulled the .38 revolver out of his jeans.

"How many times I gotta tell you? The money, drugs and guns always ride separate. One always makes the cops look for the other."

"My bad boss," T.H. said as he pulled out of the warehouse. Flea turned toward Daz as he pulled out his phone.

"Put this up," he said handing him the gun.

Flea made a quick call to Tess letting her know the van was in route. After successfully making contact he called Tony.

"What's the deal?" Tony asked.

"Not too much here. Just sent Tess a gift for Valentine's Day."

"How many karats?"

"Two. "

"Nice. I bet she'll be happy."

Tony felt his phone vibrate. He looked at the incoming call from Maine.

"Yo Flea. I got Maine on the other line. Let me get back at you."

"Peace out," Flea said.

"Talk to me," Tony said as he took Maine's call.

"Hey. You heard about Zack?"

"Nah! What's up with that clown?"

"Meka called me today and said she heard he was in the hospital, says he got hit by three slugs."

"Damn. Those niggas got beef everywhere." Tony said as he contemplated the situation.

"Shit. Whoever got him just done me a favor. You know I had his name on my whole clip."

"I know Homie, but we're on some other shit right now. We can't let small matters like that get in our way."

"It won't be in my way for long, cause I'll make that shit disappear," Maine said with a serious tone.

"Keep a level head out here. I need you, okay?"

"I'm good my G," Maine said before ending the call.

* * * *

It was 7:30 a.m. and L.G. was pacing back and forth. He had called Tweet over ten times only to reach his voicemail. He called Oak.

"Morning Boss," Oak said with sleep still in his voice.

"I'm looking for that dam boy of mine. have you seen him? He knows we gotta meeting at 8," L.G. said aggravated.

"He's at Fairview Park Hospital."

"The Hospital!" L.G. said with concern in his voice.

"He's ok, but Zack is not so lucky. Somebody shot him three times last night. No word on who or why though. Whatever went down. The streets ain't talking."

"It's that bad uh?" L.G. asked, knowing that if Oak didn't know, the situation had to be serious. "Let me find him and take care of this situation." He said as he ended the call.

L.G. walked into Fairview Park Hospital with two bodyguards at his side. He walked up to the desk where a clerk sat with a phone to her ear.

"Excuse me," L.G. said.

"One moment please," she responded while holding up one finger.

L.G. placed five hundred dollars on the desk and the clerk immediately hung up the phone.

"How may I help you sir?" she asked while grabbing the money.

"A guy got shot last night." What's the room number?"

She tapped on the keyboard a few minutes before looking up at L.G.

"Zachary Brown, room 160."

"Thank you," he said as he walked toward the elevator followed by the bodyguards.

L.G. walked into the room without knocking. Tweet was asleep in the recliner beside the bed. L.G. walked over to him and tapped him on the shoulder.

"Let's go," he said as he watched his son struggle to get up.

"Is he breathing," Tweet asked looking over at Zack.

"He'll be fine. Now Let's go."

Twenty minutes and two cups of coffee later L.G. and Tweet

walked into the Laurens County Judicial Circuit Building. The large glass windows gave a clear view to the vehicles passing outside. They walked down the hallway towards attorney client where L.G.'s longtime friend and family attorney was waiting.

"Frank Amodeo," L.G. greeted with his hand extended.

"Good Day, Mr. Goines. And this fine gentleman?" he asked directing his attention to Tweet.

"This is my son Maurice."

"Maurice," Frank said giving him a firm handshake. "Take a seat please. The both of you."

Frank Amodeo was no stranger to the courtrooms. He was one of the top lawyers in Georgia and was well respected. This case had been a cake walk for him and he was ready to deliver his expensive verdict.

"Okay, Mr. Goines I've already met with the representatives for the state as well as the judge. The defense was unable to produce any witnesses therefore the charges against your son have been dropped. The charges for Mr. Brown can be taken care of as well if that's your wish."

"Yes please," Tweet cut in.

Frank paused and waited for L.G.'s approval.

"That's fine," L.G. confirmed.

"Alright then... that's all I need from you. Maurice you're good to go but please keep yourself out of trouble. You may not be so lucky next time."

"Alright. Thank you, sir," Tweet said as he got up to leave.

"Wait on me outside," L.G. said to Tweet as he remained seated.

L.G. turned to Frank as Tweet pulled the door closed behind him.

"Thank you. My accountant will be in touch with your office soon."

"No problem Mr. Goines. Just call me if you need me," Frank said as he picked up his briefcase.

"There's one more thing I need you to do."

"What is it Mr. Goines?"

"Add Antony Parker to my retainer."

"Fax me the information and I'll take care of it."

"It'll be there today," L.G. said as he stood to leave.

* * * *

Beep - Beep - Beep - Beep – Beep!

The machine that pumped fluid into Zack's body sounded. It had been four days since the shooting. During the third operation on Zack's lower back he had fallen into a coma. Tweet watched his best friend for any signs of life as he had done from the beginning.

"I know you hear me man. You gotta wake up. We got money to make, bitches to fuck and some niggas to kill. Yeah, I know those niggas set you up. This idea could only come from that pussy ass nigga Tony. He thinks he's God now. But I got something for them. Go get well fast. We got shit to do."

Beep - Beep - Beep - Beep - Beep ....

As Tweet stood to leave the nurse walked through the door. She was short with thick hips and a beautiful dark complexion. Her short crop cut gave her an exotic look. Any other place and Tweet would have been after her number. But now wasn't the time or place.

"So, how is he doing?" she asked as she began to write down his vitals from the machine's data board.

"I guess he's okay. He hasn't moved yet."

"Well he should be coming out of it any time now. When he's up we'll be able to run more test. Right now, is just too risky"

"Has any of his family come by to visit?" Tweet asked.

"No. No one but you."

Tweet thought about Zack's family. They hated the fact that he lived the street life. They refused to allow him anywhere near their home. And promised him that prison or the graveyard would be his version of success. So Zack made money with Tweet and never offered a dime to his family. As far as Zack was concerned, Tweet was all the family he needed.

"Uh-uh-uh," Zack moaned as he began to cough.

"He's waking up!" Tweet shouted as he ran to his bedside.

"Uh-uh-uh-uh," he continued to cough.

"He needs air!" The nurse responded. "Raise the bed so that he's sitting up. We need to drain all the fluid that has settled in the back of his throat."

"Okay-okay," Tweet said as he raised the bed.

When the bed was raised and Zack's air ways had cleared, he attempted to speak.

"I can't... I can't..."

"It's okay. Don't try to speak," the nurse instructed as she watched his heart rate.

"I can't... feel... my legs! I can't feel my legs! I can't feel my legs!" Zack screamed as loud as his voice would allow.

The nurse pressed the button calling for help. Two minutes later Dr. Porter rushed into the room.

"What's the problem?"

"He said he can't feel his legs!" Tweet said in unison with the nurse.

"Young man...young man, I'm gonna need you to calm down," Dr. Porter said as he stood over Zack.

"I can't feel my legs, Doc," Zack said as he looked down at his feet.

"Listen to me," Dr. Porter said as he pulled away the sheets exposing Zack's lower body. "I'm gonna touch you okay. And I want you to nod your head yes or no if you can feel my touch. Do you understand?"

Zack nodded his head in agreement as Dr. Porter began to press him in his lower abdominal area.

"Yes," Zack responded with a nod.

Dr. Porter moved lower pressing Zack's inner growing.

"Yes," Zack responded.

"Good." Dr. Porter said. "At least we know you can still have kids."

He moved lower to Zack's thighs and gave them a squeeze. Zack did not respond.

"Can you feel this?" he asked giving Zack a hard pinch with his forefingers.

"No," Zack said.

Dr. Porter moved lower pressing his calves as well as his toes. He raised up and looked over at Tweet.

"I need to talk to him alone."

"No," Zack spoke up. "Whatever you have to tell me say it."

Dr. Porter turned his attention to the nurse. With a head nod she walked over to the machine that controlled his medication.

"Mr. Brown, you're paralyzed. One of the bullets shattered your lower vertebrae. I tried to repair it but the nerve damage was too severe.

The nurse pressed the button sending morphine into his body.

"So... so... I won't be able to... walk," Zack asked as his head begin to drop.

"No... I'm sorry... this will be a permanent way of life," Dr. Porter answered.

"There's gotta be another Doctor that can repair the nerve

damage," Tweets said. "Money's not the problem. Just get him here."

"Young man..." Dr. Porter began. "It's not about the money for me. I am one of the absolute best at what I do. I gave this young man 100% through the entire surgery. There is nothing else that can be done. Trust me I tried."

"No disrespect Dr. Porter. But you said you're one of the best. Not the best. So with that said, I'll be searching for a second opinion!" Tweet informed him as he walked out of the room.

CHAPTER 18

"T.M.G."

Tess stood in the mirror rubbing her stomach. *So this is what four months of pregnancy looks like?* she said to herself.

Tess was making more money now that Tony had taken over the organization. But this change also kept L.G. away from the office even more. After giving full control to Tony, he rarely attended the monthly meetings. With that thought, she was reminded to call Tony. She picked up her cell phone and called him.

"What's up?" Tony answered, sounding sleepy.

"Wake up. Groom-to-be. This is Tess. I've taken care of all the arrangements you asked for."

"Okay," Tony said, giving her his full attention. "There can be no mistakes, Tess. It's gotta be perfect. Now tell me exactly what you did?

"Okay. First, I had Harold's Custom Limo's reserved. After the ceremony, all black stretched Hummers will arrive on 30's to pick you and your bride-to-be up. It will take you to the W. Resorts in downtown Atlanta, where a luxury suite has been reserved for you. It's on the 26th floor overlooking the city. The room is booked for one night. The next morning, the two of you will go to the Atlanta

Airport. (Yes, it's been taken care of, Tony.) You will leave out on the 8:45 a.m. flight to Las Vegas. Upon arrival, you will have another custom limo waiting. It will take ya'll to Caesar's Palace. You have reservations for a one week stay."

"One week?"

"Yes, one week. Sorry, but Ceasar's Palace only had one week available. So that next week, the two of you will stay at The Winn. But trust me, you will not be disappointed."

"Okay. Sounds good, Tess. But what will we do? I've never been to Vegas."

"Oh, I almost forgot. L.G. has a personal tour guide there. He's been notified to make sure nothing is left unseen."

"Tess, I've always wanted to see the Grand Canyon."

"Well hurry up and say I do and you're on your way."

"Thanks, Tess. You're the best."

"I try."

"So how's the baby coming along?"

"Baby? Umm... you mean the baby?" she responded, being caught off guard.

"Yeah. You didn't think anyone noticed the baby bump you're sporting?"

"Oh, my baby. It's fine."

"What is it? A boy or a girl?"

"I haven't taken the gender test. I just wanted it to be a surprise."

"Wow. Do people even do that anymore? How does the father feel about waiting?"

"The father?" Tess mumbled.

"Yeah. You know... Baby daddy?"

"Oh yeah. Baby daddy. Well he doesn't care whether it's a boy or girl."

"That's cool. Well as soon as you find out, let me know.

I want to buy you a gift."

"Will do," Tess said, ending the call.

Tess sat on the edge of the bed heartbroken. She was carrying L.G.'s child and he wanted nothing to do with it.

"Get it together Tess," she said as she stood to get dressed for work.

* * * *

Tweet walked around the table, staring each person in the eyes. It had been two weeks since Crop had given him a direct line to all the cocaine he could sell. With Zack still confined to a hospital bed, he would be forced to build his empire alone.

"Do you all know why you've chosen to attend this meeting?"

"Yes, Boss," one of the members said.

"We do, Boss," followed another.

"To get some mutha' fuckin money," A raspy voice came from the back of the room.

Tweet looked down at the end of the table as a slim thug with Red dreads stared back at him. His cool demeanor showed he was not fazed by the fact that Tweet was in charge.

"Stand up," Tweet said, pulling his Glock 40 from his waistline. The young goon stood without losing eye contact with Tweet. "Tell me why I shouldn't blow your fuckin' face off?"

"That's easy. Because if you kill me, you won't have anyone to move all this work you're about to talk about. But more importantly, you won't have anyone to make sure you stay alive."

"And how the fuck is you 'spose to keep me alive?"

"Like this."

Tweet looked around the room and was shocked to see that pistols were pointing at him.

"See Boss, in just fifteen minutes out here with your people, I convinced them that I was your first lieutenant and that they were to answer to me and me alone."

Tweet couldn't believe this goon had the heart to pull a stunt like this on him. But one thing was for sure. He wanted him on the team.

"So, what's your name?" Tweet asked, turning his back to the pistols that was still pointing at him.

"Brisco."

"Alright Brisco, welcome to T.M.G. You'll be my first lieutenant from this day forward. Now can you tell your people to put the guns up?"

Tweet took the next four hours to form T.M G. with the help of Brisco. Tweet found out quickly that Brisco had two things that T.M.G. needed to be successful, the heart of a lion and the street knowledge to make money. He knew every major hustler that moved work in the Southeast, and Tweet listen to him as he gave advice on how to take over the streets with their new product.

"Our biggest competition is gonna be '*The Lick*.' So..."

"You know them?" Tweet asked, cutting him off.

"Never met the bosses personally. I got to meet Flea, one of the trap bosses. But never made it past that.

"How did you meet Flea?" Tweet asked in a serious tone.

"Calm down, Boss. I'm cool with one of his killers, T.H. I just happened to be in the same area one night when he was putting in work."

"Well understand this!" Tweet said, raising his voice. "I don't fuck with anything or anybody that fucks with *The Lick*. Now I need to know today. Where is your loyalty?"

"My loyalty is to T.M.G. until the day I die," Brisco said as he stared at Tweet. "The day you feel my loyalty to T.M.G. has been betrayed, don't hesitate to put a bullet in my head."

"I won't," Tweet said as he pulled a small black book out of his back pocket.

"What's that?" Brisco asked, pointing at the book.

"This is the Rules of the Game. Now teach them to everyone in this room. Including yourself." Tweet said as he handed him the book. "Make me proud," he said as he walked out the room.

CHAPTER NINETEEN

"Ghost Dope"

Tony couldn't wait for the plane to touch down in Atlanta. The wedding had been perfect, and the honeymoon was a big success as well. There was no doubt in his mind now as to the power L.G.'s name carried. Each time Mindy scanned the card, he gave her the response was always the same. *Your account is unlimited,* Tony remembered the cashiers saying.

He looked over at his new wife as she slept in a deep sleep. "Damn, I'm a lucky man," he mumbled as he laid back on the headrest and dozed off.

An half hour later, they were off the plane and in the limo headed home. Tony looked down at his phone as it continued to go off. The flight had stopped the signal from coming through. As the late text came through, Maine called.

"What's up?" Tony answered.

"I hate to spoil the honeymoon, but I need you ASAP."

"What's going on?"

"For the past two weeks the trap houses have fell off."

"What do you mean fell off?"

"The money. They ain't moving the work like they usually do."

"Maine don't panic. You're gonna have slow periods, Bra. Don't let it stress you out."

"I still have all of this week's supply with another shipment on the way."

"What the fuck!? I'm on the way. Call all the Trap bosses and meet me at the Guesthouse."

"Aight My G," Maine said, ending the call.

Tony looked at the driver. "Goines Estate," he said in a loud tone.

"What's going on?" Mindy asked, concerned.

"I really don't know right now. I need to meet with the team first. I'll fill you in later," he said as the limo pulled up to the security gate.

"This is good enough," Tony said to the driver. He leaned over and gave Mindy a passionate kiss.

"Go get some rest. I'll call you later," he said as he opened the door, climbed out and began to walk up the driveway.

As he approached the guesthouse, he pulled out his phone. Tony knew just who to call to get the information he needed.

"We're waiting," Oak said.

"I'm here. I just wanted to talk to you first to get the scoop on what's going on."

"I'm not sure yet. I've investigated several possibilities while you were gone. I'll fill you in whenever you get here."

"I told you I'm already here," Tony said as he walked through the door. Ending the call, he looked over at Oak as he continued to speak. "So does anybody have an idea as to why our numbers have fell off? Is it the product?"

"No Boss. We still got Grade A when it comes to the streets," one of the trap bosses said.

"Well what the fuck is it!!??"

"Competition," Flea said from the back of the room.

"Competition? Tony said confused. "Nobody can compete with

our product or our prices. So who's our competition?"

"Word is...," Flea said, walking to the front of the room. There's a new organization over in East Dublin. They move all their product on that side of the bridge."

"And we're losing money because of them?"

"We're at a record low," Tess said as she stepped out of the office.

"Damn, that's bad," Oak said. "Boss is gonna be pissed."

"I'm the Boss!" Tony snapped.

"So what do we do?" Flea asked.

"I say we take them out," Maine cut in.

"Why?" A voice asked from the door.

The room silenced as L.G. walked into the room. Tess's heart began to pound harder as she rubbed her swollen stomach.

"Why would you start a war with your competition? You want to know what to do?" L.G. continued as he turned his attention to Flea.

"Yeah. Tell me what to do?" Flea questioned.

"You hustle!! You hustle smarter, you hustle harder, and you hustle larger!!! When I came up in the same streets, nobody gave me shit!!" L.G. shouted as he walked around the room. "When the other hustlers shut down for the night, I was just getting started. And now you got to do the same." L.G. walked out of the room, leaving Tony to give his trap bosses their last instructions. Tony looked around the room before he began to give out demands.

"Oak. From this day forward the trap houses will run 24/7. Set up two twelve hours shifts in all of them. Bosses, you'll take the day shifts and your lieutenants will work the night shifts.

I'm gonna work on getting the prices down even more. (No guarantee there.) But let's get our numbers heading in the right direction. Any questions?"

"We good," spoke one of the Trap Bosses.

"Then let's take back our streets!" Tony said, walking around the table to give each trap boss dap.

When the room cleared out, Tony, Maine and Flea stood alone. "So what now?" Flea asked.

"What do you think? We're gonna find out who's moving that work."

"But L.G. said..."

"I don't give a fuck what he said!" Tony snapped, cutting Maine off in midsentence. "Mutha fucker's fucking with my money. I want to know who set up shop. So, let's find out."

"You know I got your back," Maine responded.

"As always," Flea added.

"That's what I'm talking about," Tony said as the crew walked out of the door.

* * * *

Flea drove down Jordan Street in East Dublin. The steady flow of dope fiends running across the streets made the drive slow. As he passed Jordan Street Projects, Flea saw a huge T.M.G. logo spray painted on the side of the building.

"T.M.G. What the fuck is that?" he asked T.H. who was leaned back in the passenger seat.

"I don't know, but I've been hearing a lot about that shit."

"Well we're about to find out."

Flea pulled the LC5OO Lexus into the parking lot of a local convenience store. They got out and walked up to a group of thugs that was busy entertaining crackheads on the backside of the store.

"Yo! what's up?" Flea said as they got closer.

"Who the fuck wants to know?" one of them spoke up.

"Shit. I'm looking for some work," Flea replied.

"I don't see no money in your hand."

"That's because the shit I carry is too much for pockets," Flea said as he pointed to the Gucci duffle bag T.H. was carrying.

The crew looked at the bag. They looked at each other with the same thoughts going through their minds.

"That won't be a good idea," Flea said, breaking their thoughts. "That money got blood on it. And if it gets taken, bodies will drop until it's returned tenfold. Trust me, it ain't worth it. Just take care of me or point me in the right direction, and I'll be on my way."

"How much is it?"

"It's enough to make your Boss stop what he's doing and come talk to me. "

"Hold on," the leader of the group said as he pulled out his phone. He walked away for a private conversation while holding his pants with one hand and the phone with the other.

Three minutes later, he returned with a piece of paper. "My Boss said to give you this."

"When do I need to be there?" Flea asked, looking down at the address.

"He's waiting on you now."

"Aight. That's a good look," he said as he pulled out a stack of money and peeled the kid off five hundred dollars.

"Let's go. We got business to take care of," Flea said to T.H. as they turned and headed back to the car.

Twenty minutes later, Flea and T.H. pulled up to the high-rise gates of Dreamers Estates, a Suburban neighborhood where only the elite live. The armed security guard stepped out of the building with his gun in full view.

"State your name and business. "

"I don't have a name, but the password is T.M.G."

"I'm sorry sir." The guard said as he pressed the security code, causing the large metal gate to slide open.

Flea drove through the gate and was shocked at what was ahead of them.

"What the fuck!" he said surprised.

"Is that the 2019 Rolls-Royce Cullinan? That shit ain't even out yet," T.H. asked in shock.

"Look over there. That's the ZR1 by Corvette. Comes out in 2019 too," Flea said, pointing at the car that had been customized with 22" chrome rims.

"There's a lot of money around here," T.H. mumbled.

"You're right. Now we just need to find out who's making it and how."

"That's the easy part," T.H. said as he climbed out the car. He walked over to a cocaine white Mercedes G-Wagon and pulled on the door, causing the alarm to go off. He repeated the process with several more luxury cars before turning back towards Flea.

"That should get somebody's attention," he said with a smirk.

* * * *

Brisco was laid back in his recliner with a blunt of the best loud hanging from his lips. He looked down between his legs and smiled as he watched his latest gold-digger attempted to swallow his dick.

"Right there, Bitch!" he moaned as he squeezed his ass cheeks together from the skills of her mouth.

Brisco closed his eyes. The high from the weed and the sensation of the blow job were about to take him over the edge, and then he heard the alarms of his vehicles going off.

"What the fuck!" he said as he climbed out the chair and walked to the window naked.

Brisco looked as two guys stood next to his cars. He immediately recognized Flea.

"Well, well, well. Look what the cat drug in. Broke mutha

fuckas must be looking for a job."

"Who is it, daddy?" The gold digger said, walking up to him to rub on his still hard dick.

"Bitch! Mind your business. Get dressed and get the fuck out," he said as he began to get dressed.

Ten minutes later, Brisco walked out the door. Flea and T.H. was sharing a blunt when he walked up.

"Who the fuck touching my shit?" he asked, walking up to T.H.

"And who the fuck wants to know?" T.H. shot back as he placed his hands inside his pants on his pistol.

"You pull that gun out and the next thing you'll touch is the walls of a casket."

"You threatenin' me, nigga?"

"Nah. I don't make threats. You better ask your Boss. I already gave you one break."

"You ain't gave me shit! Let me off this mutha fucka!" T.H. said as he looked at Flea for approval.

"Shut the fuck up, lil nigga. You can't even squeeze off without your daddy giving you permission. Now what's up?" Brisco said, turning his attention to Flea.

"You know what's up. I need some work." "Work? Aren't you with *The Lick*?"

"Shits been dry lately," Flea said, trying to keep a straight face.

"Look man. I ain't for the bullshit. You know I know that you have a plug that don't go dry. So whatever you looking for, cut the bullshit and let's get down to it."

"Aight. Since you want to put it that way, who are you working for?"

"It's not *The Lick*. So what does it matter?"

"It matters because you're fucking with my pockets!" T.H. said angrily, stepping toward Brisco.

"Oh... okay... now we're getting somewhere," Brisco said

through a slight laugh. "It's not the work. It's the money. Well let me tell you a secret. T.M.G. ain't going nowhere. And if you want to eat, this is the team to be on. Truth be told, it's just a matter of time before *The Lick* goes down in history. So the smart thing to do is jump ship before you drown."

"First of all, that'll never happen," Flea said between clenched teeth. "And secondly, you will tell me who is behind T.M.G."

"And if I don't?"

"Then the next time we meet, there is nothing to talk about."

"Is that a threat?" Brisco asked, staring Flea in the eyes.

"Nah homie. That's just my way of saying this conversation is over," Flea motioned for T.H. to follow him to the car.

CHAPTER TWENTY

"Motivation"

Zack was sitting in his new replacement for his legs, an all-chrome wheelchair with every gadget at his touch. The remote-control chair was top of the line. Tweet had made sure that nothing was left out as he attempted to make his best friend as comfortable as possible.

He looked at his spaghetti legs in frustration. "Uugghh!!!" he growled as he tried to move.

After trying over and over for the next couple of minutes, Zack swung his arms, turning over the table that held his breakfast. "Fuck!! Fuck!! Fuck!!" He shouted at the top of his lungs, causing the nurse to step into the room.

"Is everything okay, Mr. Brown?"

"He's fine," Tweet said from behind, causing the nurse to jump. "Can we have a minute?"

"Sure," she said as she walked out.

"What's up, homie?" Tweet said, looking at the frustration on Zack's face.

"Ain't shit up. Just trying to get my legs to move again. Man, I want out of this chair."

"In time it will happen. I got you an appointment with this

doctor out of Mexico. Dr. Garcia. They said he's the best. He works on all the professional athletics."

"I can't afford this shit."

"Why not? You're second in command at T.M.G."

"Yeah. But T.M.G. ain't made the first dime yet."

"Don't talk too soon," Tweet said as he opened a duffle bag filled with money. "What does this look like?" he asked as he popped the cork off a bottle of Ciroc.

"What the fuck we celebrating? My new home?"

"Nah Bra. The first day that T.M.G. made the streets, we killed the game."

"How? We're still waiting on Crop to let us know if he'll supply us."

"He called back over two months ago. You were still in a coma. I wanted to wait and give you the news when you were better"

"How much we getting?"

"Unlimited supply. Now don't worry about all that yet. Just get better."

"So who has your back? I can't help keep the wolves off you like this."

"Brisco."

"Brisco? Brisco, I've heard that name before."

"Yeah? That don't surprise me. He's a tough kid with a big heart."

"And if I remember correctly... A killer."

"I think we have the same person in mind."

"Are you sure about this?"

"He's moved two shipments already."

"Two?" Zack asked surprised.

"Yeah two. Plus, it's always better to have a known killer as your friend than your enemy, right?"

"Always."

"Now don't worry about all that. I need you to focus on getting out of this chair."

"I wish."

"I wish too. Now get some rest. You've got a flight to catch."

"Where am I going?"

"Mexico of course. Now rest," Tweet said as he turned and walked out of the door.

CHAPTER TWENTY-ONE

"And Baby Makes Three"

"Oh God!!! Don't Don't stop... don't stop... right there... right... right... there... oooh. I'm cumming. I'm cumming!!! Oooohh. Goood!!!"

Tony continued to fuck Mindy nonstop. For some reason, her pussy felt hotter and wetter.

"Damn baby!" he grunted as he released the last of his juices. "It must be getting close to that time of the month.

"Why?" Mindy asked confused.

She hadn't told Tony about the baby yet. She wanted the moment to be special. But since he'd been in the streets non-stop after their return from Vegas, they hadn't really had time to talk.

"Because it seemed like you were so hot inside."

"Well ain't that how it's supposed to be?"

"Yeah but... you know."

"I know I'm ready for another round," Mindy said, kissing Tony on the lips.

"See that's what I'm talking about. Is your period the reason you're super horny?"

"No, it's not."

"Then tell me. What's up?"

"I'm pregnant..." Tony was speechless as he looked down at his wife. His lips were moving but the words wouldn't come out. "Tony. Did you hear me? I said I'm pregnant."

"I hear you," he mumbled.

"Is that all you have to say?"

"Am I hurting you?" Tony said as he rolled off her and looked at her stomach.

"No, you're not hurting me."

"How far? I mean when did you find out?"

"Well, I'm officially three months. I found out at two. I wanted to tell you, but you've been so busy. And I just didn't want to bother you."

"Bother me. Mindy, you're my wife. You could never bother me. Never keep secrets from me, okay?"

"So does this mean you're mad at me?"

"No sweetheart. I could never be mad at you."

"Well how long do I have to wait for you to satisfy this craving?"

"Not long at all," Tony said as he climbed on top of her and let his dick slide inside.

CHAPTER TWENTY-TWO
"Real Niggas Don't Crossover. . ."

Tweet walked around the table as he continued to puff on a Cuban cigar. "So Boss, is the money still good for the person that takes out that nigga Tony?" a worker asked. "My money is always good."

"I was just wondering since we're getting money now."

"Listen! The beef I got with those niggas is deeper than the streets. Okay?"

"So what's the beef about now?" Brisco asked.

Tweet looked around at his first lieutenant as he removed the cigar.

"I pay the cost to be the Boss. So don't fucking question me," Tweet snapped as smoke streamed from his mouth.

"I'm just asking, Boss. You know unnecessary beef is never a good thing."

"You let me be the fucking judge of what's necessary and what's not. All I need you to do is keep the money coming in."

"You got it," Brisco said as he returned a stare of his own.

"I want those pussy niggas dead!! What part of that does anyone in this room not understand?"

"We got it, Boss," a worker responded. "I don't give a fuck what the beef is about. For 25 bands, those niggas can become ant food any day in my book."

"Enough said then. What's the product moving like?" Tweet said, turning his attention back to Brisco.

"The product is moving quickly and smoothly," Brisco responded, thumbing through his phone.

"Good answer. And the money?"

"It's packaged and ready to be shipped out. But you never told me where to ship it to."

"That's because I'm doing a personal delivery. Get the van ready and call me," Tweet said, walking towards the door. "Meeting over." He continued as he walked out.

* * * *

T.H. was sitting on the block, waiting on Flea when his cell phone went off. He looked down at the stranger's number.

"Who the fuck is this?" He answered with an attitude.

"Is that the way you talk to a nigga that spared your life?" Brisco said sarcastically.

"Niggas, don't spare my life. Either I take theirs or they take mine. And being that I'm still breathing, you should know who is doing the most taking."

"You ain't had this kind of beef yet."

"Spare me the tough talk and let me know why you on my phone."

"Well, I was hoping we could have a sit down. Just me and you. I want to see if we can settle this beef."

"What beef?"

"The beef your bosses have with my boss,"

"And who is your boss?"

"That's a bedtime story for another night," Brisco said with a chuckle.

"So if this beef is between the bosses, why don't we let them handle it?"

"Because if you think about it. We're the real money makers on both sides. All they do is supply the products. If this war continues, then not only is the streets at risk, but our money as well! Think, about it."

"All I know is that I'm with, *The Lick* through whatever," T.H. said in a commanding voice.

"Nigga, I ain't asking you to switch sides. I'm trying to keep the money going."

"Well if you want to keep making money, then you need to come holla at me on this side. Because as soon as we find out who you work for, you'll be out of a job."

"Don't bet your life on that," Brisco growled.

"My life's already on it," T.H. said as he ended the call.

* * * *

Brisco looked up at Tweet as he pushed his phone into his pocket.

"He didn't go for it. I knew he wouldn't. He's a street nigga, I told you."

"I don't give a fuck what he is. He's the biggest threat on that team. If we get him to join us, not only will we have the money, but will have the power as well."

"Boss. Real niggas don't cross over. They gonna ride until their death with their crew. Like me. I'm loyal to you until death. And nothing can change that. I just think you need to back off this Tony punk and focus on getting money."

"Well, I don't pay you to think. I pay you to move work and do what the fuck I say. That mutha fuckin' crew is dead! Did you understand me!!! I want that nigga's head on my trophy wall, and I will get it!!" Tweet shouted at the top of his lungs.

"Why are you so angry?" Brisco asked.

He looked at his boss as he continued to scream and shout from the mention of Tony's name. He didn't know the real beef behind the two, but he knew that if his Boss didn't gain control fast, he would lead his army into destruction.

CHAPTER TWENTY-THREE
"Do or Die"

"I don't give a fuck who the Boss is! We need to find him so I can put this to rest."

"I understand, Tony. But the only person we were able to get to was Brisco. And I told you how he tried to get T.H. to flip sides."

"Flea, listen to me. Sometimes you must outthink your enemy. Get T.H., call Maine, and y'all meet me at the Red House in thirty minutes."

"Gotcha'." Flea said as he ended the call.

Twenty minutes later, Flea turned into the driveway to find Tony waving his hand directing him to park in the back. After the vehicles was secured and out of sight, they entered the house through the rear door.

"Are we in danger?" T.H. asked as he rubbed the handle of his pistol.

"Nah... But outta sight is outta mind." Tony said as he closed the curtains. The last thing we want is for one of their people to see all our vehicles together. I have a plan and you're the key."

"Me?" T.H. asked surprised.

"Yeah. This is what we're gonna do. I want you to call Brisco back and tell him your considering his offer. You let him talk you into riding with him. Once he's done you except."

"Except! I'm with *The Lick* until I die!"

"We all know that. But they don't. You play their game until we find out who's running T.M.G., once that's done – you're out."

"I can get killed doing this shit!"

"You said you're with *The Lick* until you die, right?"

"Yeah."

"Well this is do or die. Plus, I know you can hold your own."

"Okay. I'll do it. I'll call him in the morning."

"That a bet. Now here..." Tony said as he gave everyone a new phone. "This is the new I-8 phone. it's already programmed on tracking. Just hit the map app on the screen and it will show the location of all four phones."

"Sweet," Maine said as he pressed the app. All four red dots were together, showing they were in the same area.

"T.H. once you're in good. Never turn your phone off and never leave it."

"But Brisco might question the new number. I would."

"What new number? Tony said as he called T.H.'s phone, causing both phones to ring at once." I got the basics cover. You just get in."

"No problem."

"Maine, Flea keep a close eye on him." Tony said as he headed out the back door. "We'll leave five minutes apart. I'm out."

* * * *

Tony pulled out of the driveway feeling good about his plan. He needed to get his product moving again. He thought about LG, realizing he would not be happy about his recent price drops. But if there was anybody that could let him know what was up, he knew who to call.

"Hello stranger."

"Hey Tess. What's good?"

"Nothing much. Just washing all this dirty laundry."

"Dirty laundry? I haven't sent anything to the cleaners in over two months." Tony said confused.

"Well I don't keep track of where they come from. All I do is clean them."

"Well how has the boss been acting since we're losing money."

"Losing money? Tony, who said we're losing money? I can assure you business is fine."

"But how?" he mumbled.

"What do you mean how? I've worked non-stop for the past three months. I know what's coming in."

"But it's not from me."

"What the...?"

"Yeah. That what I'm saying. I haven't turned in a full shipment in over three months."

"Well if it's not coming from you, then who?"

"That's what I've been trying to find out."

"I assumed everything went through you."

"Me too. Tess, who turns in this laundry to you?"

"I don't know. It's always here when I get here. I never see the drivers nor bosses."

"Well, all I know is someone other than *The Lick* is sending in laundry and there's only one other person to ask."

"L.G.?"

"Who else?"

"I don't know, Tony. Please be careful."

"I will. And thanks, Tess," Tony said as he ended the call.

* * * *

"This shit ain't adding up," Maine said as he listened to Tony. "I mean... We're not making a fucking dime, and the money is still coming in for LG."

"It's obvious he has another crew."

212

"But who?"

"I don't know, but I feel like if we get in with this Brisco dude, we'll find out," Tony responded.

"Have you heard from T.H.?"

"Not yet."

"My G. I feel like this nigga playing us."

"Let's keep a level head. But if that's the case, He'll definitely pay the cost."

"For sho'." Maine said as he looked at his cellphone. "Hey... I gotta take this call, G."

"Hit me later." Tony said as he ended the call.

CHAPTER TWENTY-FOUR
"Boss Call"

Mindy was walking through the mall, when she saw him. She froze in her steps without noticing. It had been months since he tried to rape her. Though he was her brother now, she still didn't fully trust him. She rubbed her swollen stomach and gave him a look.

"I got you," she said to her unborn child.

She slowly began to walk in the direction of Tweet when he noticed her. She froze again as he walked in her direction at a fast paste. She could literally hear her heart as it pumped blood throughout her stiff body.

"Mindy! What's up, sis?" Tweet said as he approached her.

He held up his hand, causing his crew to stop following him. When he was face to face with her, he looked her up and down.

"Damn sis. Somebody's been having fun without me."

"Is that supposed to be a joke? If so, it ain't funny!" Mindy said with a serious face.

"It ain't no joke," Tweet said, staring at her.

"Damn Boss. Why you ain't tell me about her. We could've been brother-in-laws," Brisco said as he stepped around Tweet to get a better look at Mindy's fat ass.

"Get the fuck back!!!" Tweet shouted at Brisco.

"Why the attitude? I just want to be a part of the family," Brisco said as he raised both hands, while backing away from Mindy.

"Don't fuck with me, Brisco!" Tweet snarled through clenched teeth.

"Alright. Alright!" Brisco said as he backed away.

"I gotta go," Mindy said as she attempted to walk away.

"Hold up." Tweet said, grabbing her by the arm.

"Don't touch me!"

"Chill the fuck out."

"What do you want. I have to go," she said as she took a step back.

"I just want you to tell, Phony Tony and the rest of that broke ass crew that if they need a job, I'm hiring. I heard things are looking pretty bad right now," Tweet said as his whole crew started to laugh.

"You are so stupid," Mindy shouted, walking away.

"I might be, but I ain't broke – bitch."

"Fuck you."

"Bitch, you should've fucked me. Then that baby would've been set for life," Tweet said as he walked off with his crew behind him.

* * * *

As Brisco walked out the mall behind Tweet, his phone went off. Looking down at the number, he knew that it was T.H.

"What's happening?" he answered as he tapped Tweet on the shoulder.

"What's good?" T.H. responded. "I just wanted to see if that offer was still good?"

"Shit, I don't know. I'll have to check with my Boss. You know they breed killers every day. Shit we might not need you now," Brisco said as he looked at Tweet for approval.

"Who is that?" Tweet mouthed without being heard.

Brisco quickly turned the phone to Tweet, allowing him to see the name. After revealing the caller, he pulled the phone back to his ear.

"So why now?"

"Shit, these niggas broke. And you know I gotta get paid no matter what."

"How do I know you ain't on some bullshit?"

"Because you know me," T.H. replied.

"This will have to be a Boss call," Brisco said still looking at Tweet.

"Well tell your Boss to get on the phone. I know he's standing there listening to the conversation."

"Still on ya' game uh, T.H.?"

"It's the only way I survive. Now tell the nigga to get the phone."

"It don't work like that."

"What the fuck you mean it don't work like that. So the nigga too good to talk?"

"It ain't that. Everything goes through me," Brisco snapped.

"Well make the fuckin' call, nigga!"

"Hold on," Brisco said, hitting the mute button.

After a few minutes he returned to the phone. "Tomorrow at 2:00 p.m. Be at my house," he said, ending the call.

"What did he say?" Tony asked as he watched T.H. pace back and forth.

"He wants me to meet him tomorrow at 2 o'clock."

"Where at?" Flea asked.

"His crib."

"Oh, fuck no!" Maine said as he stood up. "It's a trap."

"Nah. I don't think so," Tony said as he thought about the

situation. "They want protection. Every crew needs a killer."

"They got Brisco. They got a killer," Flea snapped.

"Trust me, I'll be fine," T.H. said.

"Well let's find out who's running T.M.G," Maine said as he placed his pistol on the table.

CHAPTER TWENTY-FIVE

"Safety Zone"

Tess was sitting in her office along with boxes filled with cash. She thought about her conversation with Tony. She didn't understand where this money could be coming from and at one time, LG had always kept her informed of all transactions. So if he indeed had another crew. Then who? She picked up the phone and was about to call Oak when her office door opened.

"Hello Sweetheart."

"We need to talk," she said, sitting the phone down.

"Well I'm all ears," L.G. smirked.

"I just talked to Tony. He told me that his crews isn't moving product like normal. So, if they're not making this money, where is it coming from."

"Maurice."

"Your son?" She looked shocked.

"Yeah, but he doesn't know it. He went to Crop to find a connect, not knowing that me and Crop have been friends for years. Crop called me and told me what he was trying to do.

"And you told him to supply Tweet with cocaine, all the while making him Tony's competition?"

"It's a cold world. Only the strong survive. And I must say, Maurice has impressed me with the way he built his own empire without my help."

"L.G. what you're doing is dangerous for Tony, as well as your son! Somebody's gonna get killed... But you don't care. It's all about the money with you, huh? Just like this baby. People are just pawns in your game of chess. Fuck you!!! Fuck you L.G.!!! Now get the fuck out of here!!!"

"He needed to grow up and be a man. He wouldn't listen to me, so I let the streets teach him. And as for that baby in your stomach goes, the best thing you could've done was took my advice and gotten rid of it."

"What!" Tess screamed as she jumped up, raising her pistol at the same time. "You low down, no good mutha' fuckar!"

"This is the second time you put a gun in my face. Many people don't live to tell the story after the first time."

"I ain't many people. And you of all people know this."

"Put the gun down, Tess!"

"You don't deserve to live."

"Well shoot then."

Tess centered the pistol between L.G.'s eyes. Just as she was about to pull the trigger a shadow flashed in the background. As she snapped back to reality, she realized it was Tony.

"Tess, put the gun down," he said as he slowly walked up to her. "Whatever it is. It ain't worth it."

"Don't bet on it," she said as she let the pistol go into Tony's hand.

"Crazy Bitch," L.G. said as he walked out of her office.

"What's going on?" Tony asked, looking back at L.G.

"Yeah what's going on?" Tess repeated.

"Get this bitch outta my house before I kill her," L.G. replied.

"Everybody just calm down. Give me a second, Tess," Tony

Said, walking out of her office and closing the door.

"What's going on?" he asked L.G. after the door was closed.

"The bitch tricked me man. She stopped using the pill behind my back. Now look at her. Need I say more?"

"Damn!" Tony said, thinking about the conversation he had with Tess about the baby. "It's his fucking baby."

"Don't listen to shit she says." L.G. said.

"About what? The baby?"

"That too."

"Listen L.G., Tess already told me that the money's still coming in. If I'm not making it. Then who is?"

"She don't know what the fuck she's talking about. I make more money in one day than most do in a year. I'm a hustler, Tony. You should know that by now. Look at all my trap houses and money you took. Do you think I let that stop me?"

"No."

"You damn right I didn't. I just continued to do what I do best. And that's hustle."

"Who is T.M.G.?"

"T.M.G. is a crew that's hustling harder than *The Lick* right now is all I can tell you."

"Do they work for you too?"

"No," L.G. said, looking at his watch. "If your done here, I got somewhere to be."

"We're done," Tony said, walking towards Tess's office.

He stood in the doorway until L.G. was gone. He then stepped inside the office and Tess began to speak.

"You can't trust that mutha' fucka, Tony. He's a nasty, low-down man. He tried to kill me and this baby."

"You're lying," Tony said in disbelief.

"It's the truth, Tony. I need help. I need you to protect me until I have this baby."

"But Tess, I know you're more than able to defend yourself."

"Not with a belly like this," she said as she stood up. "Tony he's trying to kill this baby."

"You gotta be kidding me," Tony said with a look of shock on his face.

"I'm serious, Tony. He came to my house a while back with two men trying to take me out because I wouldn't have an abortion."

"Tell me you're kidding?"

"I'm not."

"So what happened?"

"Let's just say they won't be able to work for anybody else."

"Well we need to keep you safe. What do I need to do?"

"Just hide me out until I give birth."

"What about this job. Who's gonna wash the money for him?" Tony asked concerned.

"Who cares," Tess said as they walked out. "This child comes before it all," She continued as they walked out together.

CHAPTER TWENTY-SIX
"Security"

Zack looked down at his legs. He was on his third month of therapy and there was no progress. The shots had damaged too much of his lower spine. "Fuck!" he shouted as he tried to move his toes.

"Is everything okay, Mr. Brown?" The therapist asked when she heard the noise.

"Why do y'all smart people always ask the dumbest questions. Do it look like everything is okay? I'm confined to a wheelchair for life. Now you tell me. You have the degree."

The slim Spanish lady looked down at Zack. He had been nothing but disrespectful since the day he'd arrived. She had researched and found out he had raped two girls back in the states. Secretly, she was glad that the doctor was unable to help him. Knowing he was leaving the next day, she eagerly answered his question in her best English.

"Frankly Mr. Brown. Me don't give a damn," she said as she walked out.

"Bitch!" Zack screamed at the top of his voice. "I'mma kill you!" He snapped. "Fuck you!"

"You've raped your last woman," she said, closing the door.

* * * *

T.H. was sitting at the table with Brisco and a few other Trap Bosses. He looked around the room. Everything was expensive. Even the girls who walked around topless.

"You can have whatever you like," Brisco said in his best T.I. voice, pointing at the girls as they passed by.

"Oh yeah," T.H. responded with a smile. "Maybe later."

"You gotta loosen up, man. It's time to live."

"I hear you."

"So where do you want to set up shop?" Brisco asked.

"I was thinking about Scottsville."

"Scottsville!" Brisco said, raising up in his seat. "Nigga, you know we don't cross the bridge with our work. Everything is done in East Dublin."

"Well I look at it like this. *The Lick* ain't making no money in the streets anymore so..."

"So fuckin what?"

"So somebody gotta get that money," T.H. said with confidence.

"That's creating problems if you ask me."

"Fuck problems! I'm with T.M.G. now. And ain't nobody gonna tell me how to get my paper."

"That's what's up. But something like that gotta go through the Boss."

"Well get him here. Everybody knows that Scottsville is a million-dollar trap spot."

"I agree."

"Well if the Boss likes money, he'll let me do my thang in my area."

"Let me talk to him first," Brisco said already planning to take this idea as his own.

"I'm about making money."

"And money we're gonna make." Brisco said as he pulled one of the girls down on his lap. "Right now, just relax and enjoy the view," he said as he pulled her panties to the side, exposing her clean shaved pussy.

* * * *

T.H. was awaken by the smell of weed and alcohol. He pushed the girl off him and immediately began to get dress.

"Where are you going?" she asked in a sleepy voice. "Come back to bed."

"You ain't ever heard the early bird gets the worm."

"Yeah. But the security gates don't open until Brisco wakes up. The whole house is secured right now. Nobody comes or goes until then. So, let's make the best of it," she said as she pulled the covers back, showing her naked body.

"Secured! Are you fucking kidding me!!"

"Not at all. Look for yourself," she said, pointing at the window.

T.H. walked to the window. He knew the house was protected by a huge property fence. But what he saw outside the window gave a whole new meaning to the word security. The security gate was covered by armed standing guards.

"Don't try anything. Please! They've been ordered to shoot."

"I don't give a fuck about them or Brisco for that matter," T.H. said as he pushed his pistol in the back of his jeans.

T.H. walked out that door, leaving the naked girl behind and walked down the hall.

"Brisco!" He shouted out. "Brisco! Get me the fuck outta here!" T.H. walked down the hallway at a fast paste. When he made it to the step's he grabbed his baggy jeans with one hand and his pistol with the other as he shouted again. "Brisco!" He walked to the entrance door only to find that it was secured by a manual alarm.

"Brisco if you don't open this mutha fucka in ten seconds, you'll have to buy a new one," T.H. said as he pointed his pistol at the door. "10 - 9 - 8 - 7 - 6 - 5 - 4."

"What's the fuck is your problem?" Brisco shouted from the top of the stairs. "Man, calm the fuck down," He continued as he pulled out his phone.

"3 - 2."

"The door is opened!"

"I'm out." T.H. said as he walked out the door.

"We have a meeting here at 12 with the Boss."

"I'll be back," he said without looking back.

* * * *

It was after two and T.H. sat at the table alone with Brisco and the rest of the Trap Bosses. They passed a blunt around while they continued to laugh and talk about the money they were making. Life was indeed good for T.M.G. and T.H. felt a hinge of jealousy.

"Where the fuck is this... Boss," T.H. said with a hint of sarcasm.

"Who the fuck is this nigga?" one of the Trap Bosses asked as he looked at T.H. with his best mean mug.

"Your worst nightmare," T.H. snapped.

"You ain't shit!" The young Boss said as he leaped out of the chair and reached for his gun.

Before his fingers could touch the handle of his pistol, T.H. had pulled his pistol and was aimed with one eye closed.

"Brisco, if you want this nigga to work tonight, I suggest you tell him to sit his pussy ass down."

The Trap Boss froze in his steps. He raised his hands as he surrendered to the gun in his face.

"You got that player!"

"I know that mutha fucka. That ain't it. If you ever disrespect me again, you gonna get fucked up – Now are we clear?"

"Yeah."

The room turned their heads around as the sound of clapping came from behind them.

"Bravo... Bravo," Tweet said as he walked towards the head of the table. "I see you still got that killer mentality," he continued as he past T.H.

Tweet stopped at the chair of the Trap Boss that had backdown from T.H. He pulled his pistol from his back.

Bac. Bac. Bac!"

"Coward ass nigga." He said as he walked to the front of the table and took a seat. "Anybody else need to leave?"

"We good, Boss." Brisco said as he fired up a blunt.

"T.H.," Tweet began, "How do I know you're gonna be loyal to T.M.G.?"

"Because I'm here," he replied still shocked that Tweet was behind the whole organization.

"What the fuck that mean. You might just be here to carry information back to that broke ass, phony Tony."

"Let's cut the bullshit! I'm here to make money. I don't give a fuck about *The Lick* or T.M.G."

Brisco looked at T.H. through piercing eyes. If it was one thing he knew for sure. It was that T.H. was telling the truth, "Let's get down to the money," he said, breaking the silence.

"Yeah! Now what's this shit about Scottsville?" Tweet asked, looking from Brisco to T.H.

"Well T.H. wanted to..."

"Let me," T.H. said, cutting him off.

"Listen Brisco told me that y'all don't move any business past the East Dublin Bridge. I think that's bullshit."

"Well for one, you don't run this. And for two, who gives a fuck what you think?" Tweet snapped.

T.H. wanted to blow Tweets head off, but he knew he had to keep it cool. He had a goal and that was to find out who ran T.M.G. Now that he knew, he just needed to get out of there without any more bloodshed. So with that, he knew the only way was to let Tweet think he was in charge.

"You're right," he said, changing his tone. "All I want to do is get paid. And Scottsville is a million-dollar spot, and my hood."

Tweet thought about the money. It was just what he needed to put him on top of his father's legacy for good. He needed this. He deserved this he thought to himself.

"You can run the operation. But I put the security team around my product."

"Deal," T.H. said, looking over at Brisco.

"I'm not fucking security!" He snapped at T.H.

"And I don't need you to be," he said as he got up to leave.

"I haven't dismissed you yet," Tweet said as he pulled out a blunt.

"I don't like smoke," T.H. said as he walked out the door.

CHAPTER TWENTY-SEVEN

"Secret Baby"

Tony laid on the sofa as he waited for T.H. to call. Mindy was in the kitchen playing around with the car seat bought for their unborn child.

"Tony?" she called out.

"Yes, baby."

"I can't get this thing to unfold."

"Did you read the instructions?"

"Three times. Now can you come... help me," she said as she leaned over the table. "Tony, help!"

"What's wrong?" he asked as he ran into the kitchen.

"Ooh God!! It's time."

"It's time?"

"The baby, Tony!! The baby's coming!"

"Oh shit," Tony shouted as he ran to her side.

"Get my bag and let's go."

Tony grabbed the bag Mindy had prepared. On the way to the hospital, he called Sarah.

"Hello my favorite son-in-law! Is everything okay?"

"AAAhhh!!!" Mindy screamed in the background.

"What's wrong, Tony!" Sarah asked alarmed.

"It's time. The baby's coming."

"Oh God!! Oh God!! Oh God!! Hurry, Tony!" Mindy screamed in pain.

"We're almost there. Hold on!"

"I can't!!! It's coming!!"

"I'm on the way!" Sarah said as she ran out of her house.

When they pulled into the emergency room entrance, Sarah was already waiting with two nurses and a stretcher.

"Hurry! Hurry!" She shouted at the nurses took command of the situation.

They placed Mindy on the stretcher and hurried her down the hall with Sarah and Tony behind.

"We'll need you to wait right here."

"No!" They both said in unison. "I want to see my baby come into the world," Tony said.

"And that's my daughter and grandchild. So, move out of the way," Sarah said as she stepped past the nurse.

"Well I guess it'll be okay this time," she said defeated.

Two hours later, Tony and Mindy were the proud parents of a healthy baby boy. Tony stepped outside of the delivery room to check his phone. He had fourteen miss calls. But they were all from Tess. He called her back. When the phone began to ring, he looked around and heard a voice behind him. He looked at a lady who was very similar to Tess.

"Is that Tess's phone?"

"You must be Tony?"

"Yeah and you are?"

"Her sister. I mean Nadine. She went into labor a few hours ago and asked me to call you and you only."

"Is she?"

"She had the baby. But we need to move her to a private room."

"Okay listen to me. That's not good enough. We have to get her to safety."

"I know. She told me about the baby's father."

"You don't know the half."

"I know if he gets his hands on this baby, it will not be good."

"You're right. Now let's make sure that doesn't happen. Come with me."

Tony walked into the room where Mindy and Sarah were sitting with his son.

"Look, I gotta go help Tess. She had the baby."

"L.G.'s gonna kill her and that baby if he gets his hands on them," Sarah said as she looked at the strange girl.

"I know, and this is Tess's sister Nadine."

As they turned to leave, the nurse walked in.

"Excuse me?" Tony said, walking in her direction. "Can we talk outside?"

They stepped outside and Tony pulled out a large bundle of cash.

"I need your help."

He told her that he needed Tess moved to a private room and placed under a false name. He also wanted all documents showing she had been in the hospital removed ASAP!!!

"Can you handle that?" he asked, handing her the money and his number.

"No problem," the nurse said as she walked off.

"Hey."

"Yeah," she said, looking back.

"If anybody. I mean anybody ask about her, call me ASAP. You got me?"

"Gotcha," she said as she stepped into the elevator.

Tony looked down at his phone as it began to beep... About time he said as he looked at T.H.'s number.

"Talk to me. And please tell me you have good news."

"Well let's just say the apple don't fall far from the tree."

"What the fuck does that mean?" Tony asked confused.

"It means L.G.'s playing us. He's been supplying Tweet the whole time."

"Wait. Tweet."

"T.M.G. Tweet Maurice Goines."

"Those mutha fuckas'!" Tony said as he heard the news. "And I bet L.G.'s behind the whole thing."

"All he's worried about is the money."

"I got something for that low life bastard."

"Nah, Homie. I got something better. Tweet just agreed to let me set up shop in Scottsville, but I have to let him put his own security there."

"How many?" Tony asked as he began to think.

"I don't know yet."

"T.H. I need you to stay put until that shipment gets to Scottsville."

"Are you thinking what I'm thinking?" T.H. asked with laughter in his voice.

"As long as great minds think alike. Look, let me call Maine. "

"I've already talked to him and Flea. And guess what?"

"What' now?" Tony asked concerned.

"Great minds always think alike. Gotta go," T.H. said.

Maine rolled Tess out of the back of the hospital. It was two in the morning and the wind was blowing steadily with a cold mist of rain.

"Hold on," Maine said as he slowly rolled the wheelchair across the street.

"Where's the car?" Tess asked.

"It's right here." Maine said as he stopped at the rental Tony had left.

"Hurry it's cold out here."

"Okay. Okay," Maine said as he cleared the alarm.

Once inside Maine headed to the condo Tony had set up for her and the baby.

"So where are we headed?" Tess asked as she cradled the child.

"Pleasant Hill. And you are not to turn off your door camera under any circumstances."

"Maine, I can handle myself. I just needed Tony's protection until I had the baby. I'm good now."

"Well things have changed a lot the past few days."

"How?"

"For one, we found out who's been turning in all the money."

"Really? Who?" Tess asked as if she didn't know.

"T.M.G. Tweet Maurice Goines."

"Fuck! That mutha fucka had Tweet set up after all he did to tear down the organization."

"So now we're going back to the old days. All deals are off."

"Is there anything I can do to help?"

"Yeah. Just take care of the girls until we return."

"The girls? What girls?"

"Mindy and her baby, Meka, Tina and Mrs. Everlyn, Tony's mother. Oh, and Mindy's mother, Mrs. Sarah."

"Where are they?"

"Everybody's at the condo."

"Maine?" Tess said with a look of sadness.

"Yeah."

"If possible. Please don't kill Oak."

"In this game, you know all too well, Tess. That in war the only way to a true victory is to take out all the enemies," Maine said as he pulled through the steel gates.

"Just try."

"So what is the little bundle of joy?" Maine asked, changing the subject.

"It's a girl."

CHAPTER TWENTY-EIGHT
"The Drop"

T.H. sat in Scottsville waiting on the shipment. Tweet had sent a full team to protect his product. A lot of the windows were still broken from the drive by that killed Dirty Red.

"This one's for you, big homie," he said as he fired up a blunt.

"Hey what time is the shipment coming?" a worker asked. "I got our people waiting."

"Well, let 'em wait."

"I got bread to make. I wish that nigga Tony would come through so I can make those 25 bands."

"25 bands?" T.H. said as he stood up and walked towards him.

"You ain't heard. Boss got 25 racks on that niggas head. Shit he can put it on all those niggas if he wants to. It's more bread for me."

"25 bands!" T.H. repeated as he grabbed his pistol. "Where those niggas live?" he asked as he caught himself.

"Shit. I wished I knew," the worker responded not knowing how close he was to death.

"If you want that nigga youngster, I'm gonna make sure you get him."

"You'll do that for me?"

"You and only you," T.H. said as he turned and walked away.

"Showtime!" He said as the U-Haul truck turned on their street.

Tweet's security team immediately posted up on the block as the truck turned into the trap.

"Get this shit unloaded A.S.A.P.!" Brisco said as he stood at the front of the truck with his finger on the trigger of his AK-47.

"I'm going inside," T.H. said. "I'll watch the storage room," he said as he pulled out his phone. He quickly found Tony's number and sent him a text.

T.H.: *Truck here. Eight heads plus, Brisco.*
Tony: *Gotcha.*

* * * * *

Tess rolled in the front door and was bombarded by the women.

"Let me see it?" Sarah said first in line.

"What is it?" Ms. Evelyn asked over Sarah's shoulder.

"It's a girl," Tess said as Sarah took the baby out of her arms.

"Go shower. We got this," Sarah ordered.

"I'll help her." Mindy said, getting behind the wheelchair.

"I think I can walk."

"Sit!" Mindy demanded as she pushed the wheelchair in the direction of the bathroom.

"Where's Tony?"

"I don't know. He just told us to stay inside until he returns."

"You know he found out your father was playing both sides."

"I'm lost. He doesn't talk to me about things like that."

"That's good. The less you know, the better."

"Ok. The water is ready. Do you need help getting in?"

"I can handle it. Thank you."

"You very welcome. Now let me go out there and try to get my little sister away from them."

"Good luck." Tess said as she relaxed her body in the warm water.

* * * *

"I want to know what room she's in now!!" L.G. shouted as he slammed his fist down on the counter.

"Sir! She's not here. We have no record of that name in our system," Nadine said as she addressed the angry visitor.

"Please don't let us find out you're lying to us," Oak said as he pulled out a stack of money. "Here. Take this. Now is there any way she could have been here?"

Nadine looked at the money. She quickly snapped back to her senses. To take the money was a death warrant for sure.

"Sir, I don't know what you're talking about. I've checked the computer and the person you are asking about has not been here. Please leave and take your money with you."

"That's fine," Oak said as he picked up the bundle of money.

"You haven't heard the last of me yet. Nadine," L.G. said as he looked at her name tag.

Nadine picked up her cell phone. She had pulled out the paper Tony gave her with his number on it. She dialed his number twice but got the voicemail. Nadine sent him a text.

Nadine: *This is Nadine. He just left looking for her... very upset.*

* * * *

Tony was waiting on the signal. He had just received a text from Nadine that L.G. was looking for Tess and the baby. Knowing that they were safe for now, he focused on the mission at hand.

"Maine. Are you in place?" he asked through the wireless earpiece.

"For sure. What about Flea?"

"I can see Flea. The U-haul just pulled off. We need to move before the workers start taking the work to the streets."

"Let's get to work then."

"North side are you ready?" Tony asked.

"North side, ready."

"South side?"

"Locked and loaded."

"Move!" Tony instructed.

The crews came up to the old building from all angles. When they were outside, they waited for the final word.

"T.H. can you hear me?" Tony asked.

"Loud and clear."

"We're waiting on your signal," Tony said as he looked down at his phone.

"Now," T.H. said as he walked to the rear door and unlocked it.

"Back door unlocked. "

"I'm almost there. Flea whispered into the earpiece.

Flea, followed by his team – crawled down the back wall until he made it to the door.

"I'm here," he whispered.

"Come in. It's clear." T.H. said.

Flea entered the building along with the team of shooters with guns loaded for war.

"Which way?"

"This way. Follow me."

T.H. lead them to a set of stairs.

"Up there." He pointed. "Stay low. You can be seen if you're not careful."

Once Flea was in place, he called Tony. "Tony we're ready."

"T.H."

"I'm ready."

Tony looked across the parking lot, "Everybody move!"

* * * *

L.G. stormed out of the hospital with Oak behind him.

"Where to Boss?" Oak said as they approached the vehicle.

"Her house."

L.G. picked up his cell phone and called Tess. After the third ring a voice picked up. "Hello."

"Who the fuck is this and where is Tess."

"You called my phone mutha fucka. Now who the fuck is this?" Meka answered, recognizing L.G.'s voice.

"This is L.G."

"And this is Meka."

"Zack's ex-girlfriend."

"No. His rape victim. Remember?"

"Okay, Meka I know those boys are stupid. But listen to me. I had no knowledge of what they were doing."

"But you protected them. Just like you did when they raped the twins. So really you're to blame too."

"So what do you want?"

"I don't want anything. I didn't call you. You called me remember?"

"I want to know where my grandchild is?"

"Really? Well you've called the wrong number to ask that. Did you think Tess had him?"

"It's a boy?"

"Yes. It's a boy. Oh and by the way you have a daughter."

"So Tess had a girl?"

"Yeah and you won't ever get your hands on it or her."

"Meka listen to me. You don't know what you're getting yourself into."

"Yes, I do. Your nothing but a pathetic killer. You kill and have people killed. And your son is just like you. And let's not forget Zack."

"You listen to me you cum drinking bitch! If you don't tell me where Tess is, I'll personally hunt you down and put a bullet in your head!"

"I wouldn't do that if I was you," A voice came over the phone.

"Who is this?" L.G. said, recognizing the man's voice.

"You know exactly who this is. Now you listen to me. If you so much as touch a hair on my daughter's head, I won't stop until your whole bloodline is extinct."

"Peter? Peter Williams?" L.G. asked in a concerned voice.

"Now that we have that out of the way."

It all made sense. L.G. thought back to when Zack was shot, and the streets didn't have a clue as to who had done it.

"Zack, that was you?"

"You know the rules L.G. Street business is street business. Family is off limits. So when he touched mine, I touched him. You do know your son was with him, don't you?"

"I do now."

"But out of respect for our past, I spared his life."

"Then I owe you." L.G. quickly chimed in.

"If that's the case, I'll spare the child's life."

"What does the child have to do with this?" L.G. asked after a brief pause.

"Because Tess is my daughter."

"But... I remember. You told me..." L.G. began.

"I know what I told you! But when you'd leave me in that trap house for days, I would trick off with a few of the fiends. And Loretta was a regular."

"Loretta," L.G. repeated to himself.

He remembered seeing her around, but he had no idea Peter was fucking her or that she was Tess's mother. Yet and still, he still had a situation to deal with.

"But Peter listen to me. I can't have this kid around."

"It's my blood, L.G. and blood is off limits. You just said you owe me a life. You've always been a man of your word. So give it to me!" Peter demanded.

"Peter!"

"Give it to me, L.G. – or we'll start a war that you know this generation ain't ready for."

"Peter!"

"Last chance, or there's no rules to the game anymore."

"Peter!" L.G. pitched as his final plea.

"Deal or no deal!"

"The child can live," L.G. said defeated.

Meka started jumping in the background as her father gave her a thumbs up. She instantly picked up the phone to call Mindy to give them the news.

"Hold on," Peter said as he ended the call with L.G.

"What's wrong now?" she asked concerned.

"I have to tell Tess she's my daughter. "She doesn't know?"

"No. That's why it was so important that I get L.G. to back off. I owed this to her. Working for him all those years made me just like him."

"Daddy?" Meka called with tears in her eyes.

"Yes love?"

"You're nothing like him," she said as she wrapped her arms around him.

CHAPTER TWENTY-NINE

"25 Bands"

T.H. walked across the floor of the building with one thing in mind. Finding Brisco. He knew that to take down a body, you must first kill the brain.

"Yo Brisco," he called out. "Let me holla at ya."

"Wha cha' got?"

"We need to go over the product again before we put it in the streets. I don't have a clear number."

"Fuck dat!" Let that shit go man. It's always been on point. Our people don't play those broke nigga games."

"Well, let it go!" T.H. said into the earpiece.

PFF PFF PFF PFF! Sounded the guns as they started blazing.

"Oh fuck!" Brisco screamed as the bullets hit the pavement by his feet.

"Get down, get down!" T.H. shouted. "Come this way!" He pointed as he led Brisco into the ambush.

They headed toward the back of the building. T.H. stopped as Brisco took the lead. When he turned the final corner, bullets ripped through his body.

PFF-PFF-PFF!

"Fuck!" He shouted from the shock and pain.

PFF PFF PFF. They continued.

"You niggas want war!"

PFF-PFF-PFF! Blac-Blac-Blac! The bullets continued to rip through the air.

Brisco barely let off any shots as his body stop responding.

The crew continued to go through the building killing everyone in sight.

"North side. Are you clear?"

"North side clear and has control of the area."

"South side?"

"South side needs back up! Can you hear me? We need help!"

"North side. Back 'em up while we secure the inside."

"North side on it, Boss."

Tony walked into the storage room behind T.H. "Everything's still here."

"Good. I'm proud of you T.H. You did well."

"Did you doubt me?"

"Never. You got Dirty Red's DNA. That says a lot."

"Yeah. I wish he could see me now."

"He does. My man. He does."

Tony opened the door to the safe and picked up a kilo. He was about to test it when shots started flying.

Blac-Blac-Blac-Blac.

'Y'all mutha fuckas want war!"

"Fuck!" T.H. screamed as he jumped behind the desk. "Get down Tony!"

Tony turned to get a look at the shooter, while reaching for his pistol. As he raised the gun, he felt the heat from the bullet as it ripped through his chest.

Blac-Blac-Blac-Blac.

"I want those 25 bands." The young goon shouted as he got closer.

"Aww shit, it's that kid Tweet offered the money to kill you."

"I'm hit T.H.! I'm hit!" Tony mumbled.

"Die nigga! Die!" The kid screamed.

Blac-Blac-Blac! He continued to shoot.

"I gotta get a shot. All I need is one," T.H. said to himself.

He looked over at Tony, and he was losing a lot of blood.

"Are you still with me, Boss?"

"I'm good. Just get that nigga."

"Yo kid. You said you wanted that nigga Tony, right?" T.H. asked as he motioned for Tony to crawl around the sofa.

"You damn right. And nothings gonna stop me. Not even you. You fucking trader!"

"I'm not a trader. It was all a part of the plan."

"Fuck you and your plan!"

Blac-Blac-Blac-Blac! He continued to shoot.

Tony made his way behind him. The shooter never saw him as he struggled to pull himself up against the wall. With blood-soaked hands, he raised the gun. T.H. looked past the kid at Tony.

"I did tell you I was gonna help you get that nigga, right?"

"Fuck you T.H.! Die slow nigga!"

Blac-Blac-Blac-Blac!

"Yo!" Tony called out.

When the kid turned, Tony lifted his body off the floor with the bullets.

PFF-PFF-PFF-PFF!

When the kid was down, Tony and T.H. walked over to his body.

"I told you I was gonna get him for you," T.H. said.

PFF.

"Maybe in the next life," Tony said as he placed another bullet in his forehead.

"You okay?" Maine asked, seeing all the blood.

"Yeah. I got hit."

"Fuck! Let's get him to the hospital."

"No!" Tony said, stopping Maine. "Don't worry about me. T.H. get me to the car. Maine you and Flea make sure we get all the product. After that's done, burn the place to the ground," he instructed as he threw his arm around T.H.'s shoulder and stumbled out.

CHAPTER 30

"PROFIT"

Tony leaned against the wall as T.H. banged on the door. "Mindy! Sarah! Open up!"

"Who is it?" a voice said from inside.

"It's me T.H. Tony's hurt."

Sarah pressed the code to free the locks. She opened the door.

"Oh my God!!!" She screamed.

"What is it?" Mindy asked, running to the door. "Tony!" She shouted.

Mrs. Everlyn grabbed her son and helped T.H. get him on the couch. She looked around for something to stop the bleeding.

"Get me some towels and cold water."

"We have to get him to a doctor," Tina said.

"No," Tony and his mother said at the same time.

"Just get the towels," Tess said.

Everlyn and Tess cleaned the gunshot wound as the rest of the girls looked on in tears. Tess packed the wound with gauze.

"Is he gonna be okay?" Mindy asked.

"Of course," Tess said. "He's a survivor."

"Mama," Tony said as he cringed from the pain.

"I'm here. I'm here."

"Where's my son?"

"He's here," Mindy said as she held the baby.

"Give him to me."

Mindy placed the child on his chest as he laid on the sofa. Tony and his son stared at each other until they both fell asleep. Tess walked over to Mindy.

"You never told me his name."

"Profit."

"And your daughter?"

"Joy."

Mindy looked over at her sister. Sarah was holding her while Everlyn watched.

"Are they really gonna fight for them forever?" Mindy asked.

"Only for the next eighteen years," Tess said as they both shared a much-needed laugh.

"I say we take advantage of this and get some rest."

"I agree."

They walked to the bedrooms, leaving the women to watch the babies.

* * * *

Tweet pulled up to Scottsville. He couldn't believe he had let T.H. get inside his organization.

"How the fuck did he get in?" Zack asked from the passenger seat. Tweet had just picked him up from the airport. He'd just returned home after learning the operation was a failure, and he'd be bound to the wheelchair forever.

"Brisco."

"You mean Brisco. The kid you told me about?"

"Yeah he knew T.H. and wanted to let him join our team. He only played us. Yeah, and this place got burned to the ground.

I know that nigga Tony got that shipment of cocaine."

"So what do we do now?"

"We..." Tweet paused when his phone went off. "Hello pops," he said, looking at the caller I.D.

"What the fuck happened!"

"What do you mean?"

"My fucking product. Crop tells me you lost a whole shipment."

"Crop?" Tweet asked confused.

"You fucking right Crop. Where did you think he got the shit from?"

Tweet was furious. He'd been played by his father again.

"So you had me working with that nigga."

"I didn't have you doing anything. You came to me."

"I had no idea you were behind Crop."

"You didn't ask. I was actually proud of you. You shut his organization down on pure hustle. Son that's all I ever wanted. I knew you had it in you."

"Yeah, but you were too focused on that nigga Tony to see my hustle."

"No son. You were too caught up in your feelings about your own sister to think straight."

"Fuck that bitch and fuck Tony. I took the streets from that nigga!"

"Now that you have them what are you doing with them?"

"I'm gonna find that nigga and make him and his family pay for this shit."

"No son. That's not why I called."

"Why not? I gotta get this product," Tweet said confused.

"Fuck the product. You'll have another one tomorrow."

"Tomorrow?"

"Or today? Just promise me you'll hustle and take care of business like you ran T.M.G.?"

"Alright pops."

"No more war?"

"No more war." Tweet said as he ended the call.

Zack heard the whole conversation. He turned to his lifelong friend.

"Are you really gonna let that nigga get away with this shit?" he said, looking at the smoking ashes.

"Would I do some shit like that?" he asked as he pulled off.

"Not in this lifetime," Zack said as they held their pistols out the window firing off shots.

Blac-Blac-Blac!
Blac-Blac-Blac!

* * * *

Tess was all packed and ready to go. Tony bought her a new car and had it stuffed with things for her and Joy.

"Well you're all set," Tony said, giving her a hug.

"All I need now is Joy," Tess said, watching Meka give the baby goodbye kisses.

"Give her to me," Sarah said as her and Everlyn waited their turns.

When they were all done, Tess placed Joy in the car seat. "Take care and be safe," Maine said as he stood beside Meka.

"Take care of my niece," Meka said.

"At all cost," Tess said as she held up the chrome 45 with pink grips on the handle. "I ain't got time to play with those niggas. Right Tina?" she said with a wink as she pulled off.

They all waved goodbye as Tess drove away. Sarah and Everlyn turned at the same time, when they heard Profit's cry. Mindy turned but Meka grabbed her arm.

"The grandma duo got it," she said, and they all started laughing.

They walked back inside the house and watched as the

grandma's spoiled Profit. Tony walked around the room, stretching his stiff arm.

Ding-dong ding-dong the door sounded.

"I wondered what she forgot?" he asked as he walked toward the door.

Tony opened the door and saw a vase with flowers on the steps. A huge black card was clipped on the side of the vase.

He looked around to see who they were from. "Somebody left flowers," he said, picking them up.

He opened the card and it read, *See you in Hell Phony Tony!!!*

Blac - blac - blac - blac - blac!

The Lick Pt.2
Profit

Coming Soon.

ABOUT THE AUTHOR

Nico Harswell is a true Georgia native who proudly writes about his city and state. He was born and raised in Soperton A.K.A "The Box". Wanting to experience what the streets call the good life; Nico took to the streets at the early age of seventeen where he began his journey in and out of some of the roughest prisons Georgia had to offer. Nico knows firsthand how the cold streets will suck you in and drain years of life out of you in what seems like seconds.

It would be prison where he discovered his love for writing. Now with Georgia Boi Publications, Nico can continue to flood the streets with his product. Look forward to seeing him on every street corner as he continues to supply you with that Grade A!

We Help You Self-Publish Your Book

Made in the USA
Columbia, SC
22 May 2023